MADRID WILL BE
THEIR TOMB

Elizabeth Duval is an author and the spokesperson for Feminism, Equality and LGTBI+ rights for Sumar. In 2020 she published *Reina*, the first memoir in Spain by a woman from GenZ, as well as *Exception*, a verse poem. In 2021 she published the essay *Después de lo trans* and the novel *Madrid será la tumba*. In 2023 she published *Melancolía*, a sociopolitical essay on how to recover hope when facing a grim future. She is also a regular contributor for national media outlets like eldiario.es, Público, El País, and La Sexta.

Alice Banks is a translator from Spanish and French based in Madrid. In December 2022, Alice's translation, *Deranged As I Am*, by Ali Zamir, was published by Fum d'Estampa Press. When she is not translating, Alice also works as a publisher at Fum d'Estampa Press and an Editorial Assistant for The European Literature Network, where she writes the monthly column, 'La Española'.

This translation has been published in Great Britain
by Fum d'Estampa Press Limited 2023
002

This edition is published by arrangement with
Elizabeth Duval c/o MB Agencia Literaria S.L.

English language translation © Alice Banks, 2023

The moral rights of the author and translator have been asserted
Set in Minion Pro

Printed and bound by Great Britain by CMP UK Ltd.
A CIP catalogue record for this book is available from the British Library

ISBN: 978-1-913744-39-7

Support for the translation of this book was provided by Acción Cultural Española

MADRID WILL BE THEIR TOMB

ELIZABETH DUVAL

Translated from Spanish by

ALICE BANKS

Against anti-fascism, fascism. Simple.
MELISA DOMÍNGUEZ RUIZ

Desire can never be deceived. Interest can be misguided, misunderstood, or betrayed, but not desire. Hence the cry of the Reich: no, the masses were not deceived, they desired fascism, and that needs to be explained.
GILLES DELEUZE AND FÉLIX GUATTARI

I need you Spain, all of you; / giant quartz, thick forest, stone; / complete heaven of hearts / in sorrow. / I need you Spain / unanimous and whole / like the cry of the wind / on the great sea. / Not your Spain or my Spain. / Our Spain! / Honest terrain, carrying the joy / of maternal integrity. / Because all are children of your flesh and blood, / dreams of your vigil, knives of your sail.
VICTORIANO CRÉMER

If I had bloody thoughts in my head, the whole universe would die. It would be like volcanoes were erupting everywhere. [...] ETA is the true and only opposition there is against the government. [...] Long live intelligence and long live death.
LEOPOLDO MARÍA PANERO

He needs violence to abolish violence, [he believes] that the objective of history is to end history.
HANNAH ARENDT

PART ONE:
ENVY

Something spread through Madrid like a parasite, swelling its arteries with cement and burning in the air; beneath the garish plastic metro tunnels, a poison met another poison. They called the building containing a world on the brink of explosion the Castillo. In the entrance there was a food bank and a cloakroom; on the spacious first floor, a myriad of bedrooms and rooms; the second floor was divided into the meeting room, the library, the living room and the kitchen; the third and final floor was home to more bedrooms and a balcony from which they could gaze down upon their territory with a belligerent spirit. From the rooftop, the map stopped and started. Madrid was filthy, a city bent on self-destruction: it contemplated itself in the mirrors of Sol's metro station entrance – whale-like, almost cubist – and cracked its knuckles. The distribution of its roofs was chaotic, its joints were dirty, and in each tiny fragment of cluttered buildings, one could make out as many copper tones as the elements had been able to establish as they scorched existence, now burnt to a crisp. In the centre everything was compressed and squeezed between tiny buildings – Madrid was nothing but a Manchego *pueblo* suffering from acromegaly – while in the North, where the four towers dominated, everything became something else. These rich neighbourhoods were those into which parallel worlds did not venture, and though the borders separating them were delicate, the flows between districts were but an illusion. The threat of invasion loomed over every public space, and none could escape its clutches. The phenomenon was neither as magnified as in Las Lonas, nor did it languish like on the great Parisian boulevards, but misery and opulence occasionally came to share a corner, each being fully aware of the other's will to put an end to their existence. The extermination of the social class to which they did not belong was on the mind of every good *madrileño* – this thought being precisely what distinguished them. There were large, bona fide wastelands: territories that belonged to some (for use) only to be later bought by others (for money). These were territories on which nothing had been constructed, they simply served as spaces for conspiracy. The Mercado de la Cebada had not yet been refurbished, nor had it been invaded by the kitsch and colourful winds announced by the movement of clouds, lanterns, and garlands. The people drank their cans of Mahou beer and drank, waited, lived on, and drank until they died. Crossing two streets and heading down the hill, you came to the Glorieta de Embajadores where the abandoned waited for someone to drag them away and desert them, for an act of kindness, a miracle. That neighbourhood still believed that the world was on the verge of change, but its hopes grew smaller day by day. There were those, too, who had never even considered hope: those who drifted in and out of the public showers in the Casa de Baños with sores in their mouths and blood on their hands. They had no time to think, so they didn't; they had no money to live on, so they didn't. They held up as best they could and resisted, they didn't dream. If they so wished, they could enter the Casa de Baños where their whims were reduced to the choice between hot or cold water, better facilities, or a little warmth. They didn't vote in the last elections, and they faced the next ones with indifference. They got involved in politics the only way they knew how: by shutting up. Politics, like everything, consisted of managing spaces in specific ways: an administration of the world and of the people. National governments could distance themselves from the specific and proceed thanks to abstraction, while local groups could not afford such disconnection. Politics was the management of human loneliness, and there were individuals who clung to political groups in order to find a cure for this loneliness, like an addict or a libertine who needed another fix. The greater the feeling of doing something good for the surrounding community, the more importance the addiction was charged with, thus greater consistency and commitment was required. In Madrid, as the city turned on itself, some cultivated conspiracies of new, different worlds in their hearts: it was like this in the north of the city that plundered and the same in the south that doubled over and grinded, even more still where both trenches met. At half past four in the morning the doorways of Calle del Oso filled up with aluminium and heroin while the starry-eyed yearned. There were plenty of streets in Madrid that were full of shame, but none stooped lower than Gran Vía, where death was ready to be received between the cars and the *boina* of smog that swelled and gained strength. There were bridges and streets that no one should have to travel at night; Madrid was a city of more than a million slowly rotting corpses that no one questioned, because whoever brought it up would sacrifice their own conscience. But in its eyes, Madrid was more vibrant than arid and devastating: its malice was forgotten with the night, as crimes that no one wanted to remember are forgotten. Madrid brought up this century's youth with the greatest generational shame, instilling even their victories with nihilistic spirits: things were not, nor could be, nor would ever be otherwise. When the sun set on their anger, everything would continue to be in the hands of the same men, consumed by the same teeth.

Will you forgive me if I force you to relive it, to go through that painful story once more? It rose from between the ruins of two abandoned buildings, when some of us still believed that everything was about to change forever, and we found that the change had only been a spasm, an ellipsis, a comma. Madrid, if it were to consider its subjects, would determine that it was convenient for their imagination to be pious... very little remains of a tale of morality when morality has turned its back on it.

Curse his naïveté: Santiago hadn't thought that when Alejandro suggested opening a toy bank alongside the traditional food bank, that it would end up being him – as if he were just another militant activist, just one more pawn – waiting around for a certain *javio75* at the mouth of the Avenida de América metro. Just a few days earlier, the aforementioned had posted a listing on Wallapop: 'Sparkle Girlz pool party, almost new'. It wasn't his only offer, he'd also snuck in a second ad – 'Sparkle Girlz hold my hands and sing with me doll' – which was in direct competition with another on the free market – 'Sparkle Girlz floral fuchsia fairy'. Given the organisation's inability to get a hold on their expenses, and taking into account that negligible donations were the only thing that made their day-to-day running possible – the small to mid-size investors who continued to promise they would emigrate from some already senile organisation still hadn't fulfilled their promises – the Captain had introduced a new, fundamental doctrine: they were to save every last cent. They couldn't waste a single euro in vain, they weren't to touch the money in the pot, they couldn't even buy sunflower seeds with the shrapnel found down the back of the sofa. The toys they had already received in the form of gifts or donations were not enough to cover what they would need according to their latest predictions, and they would have to add to what they'd already collected with whatever they were selling in the Bazaars, in Carrefour, or on second-hand sales apps. Borja, who arrived at this decisive meeting five minutes (no more, no less) before it started, took care of picking up some footballs and a game of Hungry Hippos; Santiago took care of the girl's section and made self-sacrifice a capital virtue.

How had he got here? Santiago was an activist. To be an

activist meant to obey something greater than oneself. To live meant to take sides. To be an activist meant to be a partisan. Those who were indifferent or apathetic were parasites, cowards, lifeless. Indifference and apathy were diseases of the bloodless. All good parties were divided into two groups: propagandists and activists. Santiago was a propagandist who, that night, had been exceptionally forced into playing the role of an activist. To be an activist meant to obey something greater than oneself. That 'something' could be God or any other religious idea. Imperfect beings needed perfect ideas to cling onto. The idea in itself could vary, but the underlying relationship or mechanism remained. And that mechanism, once activated, could not be stopped without external intervention.

How had *javio75* got here? Santiago guessed he was about forty years old, divorced, and with, he reckoned, one or two daughters as a result of his failed marriage. He was probably right, he thought, as you could work out a lot about someone from just their name. His password was probably his ex-wife's address – the most recent, of course, he would update it every time she moved – and the year they got married. He was a stealthy voyeur, wary, yet with a password that was susceptible to being cracked. He looked violent, Santiago could imagine him cutting the telephone wire with a carving knife and being predisposed to silencing and threatening. He was able to deduce all of this from just the thickness of his beard. Santiago took solace in their lack of resemblance: he, on the other hand, was clean shaven, taller, more or less in shape, his eyes perpetually edging towards intimidation. But nothing about this bum's appearance answered Santiago's fundamental question. Nothing seemed to offer the answer as to why a middle-aged man was selling two 'Sparkle Girlz' toys on Wallapop on the 5th of January, the night the Three Kings came to deliver presents to the children. Santiago remembered that the ads had both been up for a few days. He guessed that this guy didn't have a family or, failing that, that the absence of his family must be recent, but not so recent that he hadn't already had time to go through the necessary stages of grief. Unless he was a psychopath of course, someone capable of selling his little daughter's toys just one week after her death, an opportunist, a man with a shark-like mentality, immune to everything, incapable of falling ill (not even mentally). Cancer. Carcinoma? What was it called, the one that affected the blood cells, not the tissue? Leukaemia, the disease of the bloodless. How many children died of leukaemia every year? He could imagine the little girl with her small, smooth, round head like a white billiard ball, despondent after all the chemical blows she had received, all the serology, just hoping to spend her next year in peace. He saw her father preparing her presents. No luck, next time. Demographics had to remain more or less balanced so the earth didn't overflow with souls. Maybe cancer, carcinoma, illness was not the answer, maybe the man had killed the girl and his wife after catching the latter in bed with someone else: a crime of passion committed in a jealous rage. The gift would have already been purchased before the idea of killing mother and daughter entered his mind. It hadn't even been an idea; it had been an image, an impulse. Ideas could just *come* to us, but images were provocative, producing vomiting, nausea. Violence was not an idea – Santiago made a mental note –, violence was a force that didn't stop, like the mechanism that once activated… The idea of this man killing his wife and daughter – he thought about whether *idea* was the right word to use in this sense, and decided it was – was sickening. If it were down to him, he wouldn't buy a 'Sparkle Girlz' toy from *javio75* and thus, in a way, financing his wickedness. But the decision was not Santiago's to make. A new hypothesis came to him, one that allowed him to continue with the exchange. He imagined him as a degenerate of another kind: a pervert who was anxious to get rid of his fetish, the origin of his fixation; another male posting photos on Reddit of dolls covered in semen after they'd wanked all over them. The sparkly nymph in her swimming pool was blonde and svelte, almost anorexic; she wore a one-piece swimming suit that didn't show any cleavage – she was flat, no breasts. Her face was strangely mature, but it was clear she used anti-wrinkle cream and was in the habit of drinking smoothies. She wore a pair of heart-shaped sunglasses: pink, rose-tinted. She must have excited *javio75*. Remembering the second ad, Santiago didn't want to think about what this creep was capable of doing with the other doll in front of him, the one with the hands, the singer. The size of her hands, the unpleasant sensation of plastic against skin. He thought about sterilising the toys before they gave them to the children. Things wouldn't have been so complicated had he been able to deal with the Hungry Hippos: no old man would play with himself so he could ejaculate over some hippos – maybe horses or ponies, but hippos? However, any man with perverse sexual fantasies would be capable of getting off over a Bratz doll. He wondered, for a moment, if he was projecting his own perversions onto poor *javio75*. He dismissed this idea immediately: he had never felt excited by a doll; when he was younger, he would always satisfy his compulsions by rubbing himself against the pillow on his bed, or with the help of a sock: more noble instruments, utilitarian, simple. The exchange was also utilitarian and simple. Santiago took the box, stuffed it into a green plastic bag, took the money out of his pocket and slipped it into *javio75*'s hand without even glancing at him. They said thank you and wished each other a good night.

Happy Three Kings night. He thought – like anyone just thinking about anything – about the affection that existed between Primo de Rivera and Lorca, about how much they shared, including their love for monarchy. Some verses came to his mind: *si tu madre quiere un rey, la baraja tiene cuatro: Rey de oros, Rey de copas, Rey de espadas, Rey de Bastos / if your mother wants a king, the deck has four: King of Spades, King of Hearts, King of Clubs, King of Diamonds*. Santiago thought that guillotining monarchs had always been a good idea: making those Saharan mirages vanish with a sharp blade, wiping out those stars without auras, men without auras, the living dead. Unfurling an exasperated nationalist flag with Jacobin ardour and hoisting it, raising it from the tracheas of those deformed, consanguine eunuchs meant that the standard flew brilliantly, proudly. Spain's current king and his father reminded Santiago of the gentlemen whose houses his mother had always cleaned, those houses filled with so many books, yet devoid of love. Rich houses always had so much space, and they sometimes even voted for *socialist* parties. Those defenders of the demi-bourgeois system could afford to have expansive corridors that joined rooms together; they no longer practised any quintessentially Spanish eclecticisms, nor were they capable of decorating different rooms as if they were of different eras. A new and singular *malasañismo* – a surge of middle-class, hipster socialists in the Malasaña neighbourhood – now prevailed as an aesthetic and consisted of two sides. This central neighbourhood of the city, once the heart of the debauchery of *la movida madrileña*[*] was now home to two kinds of socialist. The first was poor, added as a subcategory some time ago (amongst speakers of the perverse newspeak, the proletariat had been replaced by the

[*] A countercultural movement that took place in Madrid (and other Spanish cities) during Spain's transition to democracy after the death of dictator Francisco Franco in 1975. It saw a rise in punk rock and synth-pop music, and an openness regarding sexual expression. The aesthetic became embedded in the city's fashion and art and also effected an emergent LGBTQ+ community. Whilst many people involved in the movement declared there was not a unifying political ideology, many elements of the movement were antifascist and had anarchist leanings.

precariat, that is, the decomposing middle class); they all had the same furniture, it was all too easy to trace its origin to some huge, concrete, homogenous IKEA building on the outskirts of the city, thanks to those who had forgotten to tear off the labels. Then there were those who weren't poor – those sons of bitches – who ordered their furniture custom-made, commissioned interior designers, assessed their options, saved money, and even allowed themselves to go over budget. The poor bought 'Sparkle Girlz' or whatever other crap they could afford, and the sons of bitches ordered their artisan toys, designed sensory tables, and took their children to Montessori schools – they wanted to develop their intelligence but, most importantly, they didn't want them to mix with outcasts of a different ilk, of a class too far below them. Santiago had never believed in those myths. For him, it was but a question of genetics, a Spanish issue, a race issue. Lola Flores once said that the reason she was so beautiful was because one can't change the whites of their eyes, because what one feels on the inside always rises to the surface. Those idiots could hide under as many palatable layers as they liked, but they would always be insufferable, arrogant cokeheads, worshippers of the state, believers of progress who were dizzy from so many turns of the spinning top, despite being the ones that always pulled the strings. Happy, radiant, they were always families and never collectives, always conservatives, progressives, and never revolutionaries. They were chameleons, capable of going to sleep as one thing and waking up as another. They were savers and lovers of overspending with no need for money, no need to study, soulless, lifeless, exhausted, but apparently happy, wrapped up in their own little worlds. They were vultures who reaped the rewards of so many other peoples' work, scavenging from hands and bodies that broke every day. The Castillo had declared war on them. None of them would bring their children to try the supermarket bought Three Kings Roscón tonight. If being an activist meant anything, it meant being a voice for the mute, a shelter for the homeless.

Come and get some Roscón. Let's share the cake, and with it, happiness, and with happiness, patria! There was no evil to be found within the eyes of the parents that brought their children that evening. Tears, Santiago had always thought, looked so much like drops of blood, because they purged the deepest suffering and pain, they exorcised one's true feelings. Santiago watched gratitude light up the eyes of the parents that had brought their children to the Castillo that evening, making everything worthwhile. They wouldn't have come if they had any other means. Would they eat something so disgusting if they could afford something else? They didn't even take off the slices of candied fruit, and the green pieces were revolting. Long live the King of Spain.

No matter how much power he had, Santiago knew his opinion was not the majority within the organisation and so he had to coexist with the others and learn to bend to them. Ideological diversity had always been a virtue of the organisation. The Captain repeated insistently: *it doesn't matter where we come from if our objectives are the same.* Who, apart from her, did he trust? He knew that his Three Kings were the Nation, the Republic, and Nationalism: the patria, work, bread and butter. In another time they would have wielded swords and hammers together. But they covered up any signs of ideology that were too obvious and tore down all the usual symbols. *We will not be able to carry out our campaign, nor will we achieve victory with outdated declarations...* Who had said that? They had had to learn to exist in hostile territory, where a reaction appeared long before the seed had even been sown. *Charge, free citizens! Long live the legends that can only be sustained in war, violence!*

There was no violence in giving bread to someone who arrived with empty hands, but there was a construction of legacy, there was love. *We're establishing a community*, the Captain would say, and in doing so they were choosing those who belonged to them, to the organisation.

Everyone in the organisation had a least a few things in common, they all led more or less similar lives, and they all chose the same animals for company. No one in the entire organisation had a cat. The presence of cats – which were already considered a plague or infestation in places like Cyprus – was seen as the first sign of degeneration. Their treats also contained cereals, meats, animal by-products, oils and fats, mineral substances, vegetable by-products, palm oil, death oil. Dogs, on the other hand, protected: they were neither pets nor were they submissive, but rather comrades, tools, shields, and arms; they were just the same as the poor, the outcasts, the famished, those who arrived at the building with their children and saw toys, food, paradise: they were loyal.

Whilst Christian charity may have served as an inspiration for the organisation, their reasoning was not neo-catholic: *if we control the flow of what they put into their mouths*, said the Captain, *we will also control their aspirations, their desires, their goals and objectives, their collective vision of the world and things.* Those who controlled what someone put into their mouth also controlled their fingers, their teeth, their gums, their jawbone, their mandible.

Santiago would have also added that those who dominated dreams held even more power – almost like a child's inseparable bond with a blanket, a stuffed toy. There was something genuinely moving about the way in which the Captain took the children in her arms or by the hand and lead them to Juanma, or 'King Melchior'. Most of them were quiet as she called out the names of the children one by one. They then received a present, posed for the camera, and picked out another present from the pile of leftovers. For a moment, Santiago forgot about the repulsive force that made him distance himself from the others. *Emilio. Aitana. Hello Aitana! We're going to get a little present, then take a photo, get a little present and then take a photo with our flag in the background, our flag with our logo, so beautifully drawn, a fortress and the* madrileño *bear, a photo whilst you suck your thumb, who isn't going to love your adorable little face?* The faces were familiar. The poor were multiplying, and those who were already poor continued to be so. The mechanism, once activated, could not be stopped without external intervention. *Hello Gabriela!* He supposed that everything was worth it. Who in this place right now wasn't momentarily happy, infected by the joy of others? *You can choose whatever present you like, little champ... but don't go picking one of those girly ones. Here, Tristan, here you go. Don't want that one? No? Do you like the rocking horse? Bye bye! How old are you, Diego? I'm going for a smoke. Daniela. You're called Daniela? Daniela! And how old are you? Have you been a good girl this year? You've been very good. The best. What's your name? Jorge. What team are you? Real Madrid! Olé! Vamos! Well, you can pick whatever you like.*

Santiago realised that he had been a miserable child: the capital city inoculated diseases like that, converted children into ungrateful beings, transformed poverty into a genetic issue, prepared kids for hate, for the worst, for despair. When he was eight years old, his father gave him a book on the 6th of January. A book did not cost the same as a toy, a book was worth nothing, and if it was bought from the supermarket then it wasn't even a sign of class, rather turning on itself and becoming a source of shame. He screamed and cried at not having received real presents like the other children, for having to go to school and being left out for 'bragging' about a stupid little green book. A father shouldn't clean graveyards and smell like shit. He wondered if he had inherited the stench. He contemplated the room for a little longer before going outside to smoke as he waited for the farce to come to an end.

Let's add a little nuance here. Santiago didn't hate his comrades so much, not in excess; his discrepancies, even with the thugs, were more to do with small ideological disagreements, different ways of doing things, different methods of working things out. He knew he was obnoxious, but in that moment, seeing the children's faces filled with joy, he supposed that the ungrateful soul he was in childhood could be redeemed by his current work. He didn't identify with misery's most common feeling: a feeling that led someone to believe that as they didn't possess something, nor could anyone else, a feeling that led people to want to extend their shortcomings to the rest of the world; he reminded himself that envy was one of the seven deadly sins for which one's bones would rot. He did then, what he would have liked someone to do for him as a child: he wanted to take care of others as he imagined they would have taken care of him. His project was not limited to just this, however, it was much more than that: it was a general extension of heaven's kingdom, its enormous expansion over everything.

A while passed before the Captain came out onto the balcony. Santiago thought back to their never-ending nights of conspiration just two years earlier: actions before words, ideas calculated by the exact measure of their effects, the radical transformation of the world always before discourse and never vice versa. He saw their figures from behind: the bandage on her ankle covering her permanent, imagined wound; the bomber jackets he wore, elongated and slender; their territorial footprints. He thought about the whiteboards and the calendars,

23

about the mathematical control of those days, the coups, the revelations, the narrative construction of the world. That night, as he watched the Paseo de Castellana light up with the parade and contemplated the passage of the Three Kings that were even more false than theirs, he thought for the very first time that the script he had written might fail; he considered the possibility that someone could snatch the baton from his hands.

They didn't get the chance to exchange even a single word, as the Captain didn't give him the chance to greet her warmly. Santiago stamped out his cigarette, well-consumed, and went back inside the Castillo.

On the floor of solidified beer, a toilet; on the toilet, a lid; on top of the lid, someone was cutting some lines – ill defined – of speed. Ramiro didn't get involved the first two times as he still hadn't drunk enough, but the third time around he accepted whilst someone lit up the bathroom with the torch on their phone. Fumbling, he rolled up a five euro note, bent down and rose back up. The volume of the music that came from the floor below was insalubrious, that place too, that place was insalubrious, every wall was covered in graffiti that no one at such an hour was capable of reading. The living regarded each other with both respect and disdain, in the same way one would look at an ally. They went back downstairs hoping that the guitars would transform into something else, that the performance would stop, and that someone would appear on the decks. A crowd of bodies into which one could dissolve rhythmically moved their heads, their arms, their hips. Tired, yet awake, Ramiro went outside to smoke and find his friends. He thought about the rest of the teenagers – because that's all they were – who had risen from the swamps; he thought of all the drugs that simultaneously invaded their bodies. He stepped outside and bought a can of beer, taking advantage of the fact that a *latero* was passing by selling them. He stopped thinking, sat down, and listened in on the nearby conversations.

Ramiro was an activist. To be an activist mean to obey something greater than oneself. To live meant to take sides. To be an activist meant to be a partisan. He hated those who were indifferent, but he was incapable of feeling contempt towards these parties, even though they made him sick. They served to finance other issues: the *okupa*'s* office, the self-run library, the sign language courses, the solidarity coffee shops, the resistance against gentrification. These parties, however, were also spaces to which just anyone came to get fucked up.

He looked back over at the *latero* and wondered if he was Indian, Pakistani, or North African. He immediately regretted that the first thing that had come to his mind was to categorise him, box him in, think about his origins: a coloniser's taxonomy. He realised that he was incapable of exchanging many words with him, as they came from different worlds, and maybe they didn't even share a common tongue. If Ramiro spoke to him about 'precariousness', or even worse, 'the class fight', the *latero* would likely send him most splendidly to hell.

Vero, who Ramiro knew well – they were activists together – made the most unexpected of movements, a subtle twist of a few degrees, and struck up a conversation with the guy. It turned out he was from Bangladesh, his name was Abdul, and he expressed himself relatively fluently in Castilian. Much to Ramiro's surprise and shame, Vero knew who he was: the *latero*'s union meetings took place in the same occupied house in which he was partying. They spoke of the pittance that Abdul earned each night, and how the sales of the beers barely covered the fines he got.

Ramiro didn't live far from Plaza Nelson Mandela, whose name he still couldn't get used to, so as soon as the police arrived, he thought about leaving. The music stopped and everyone fell

* 'Squat' or 'occupied house/building'.

silent, sat down, snuck out. But none of them were going to have to deal with the police, they'd come for the *lateros*, for the Senegalese guys camping out in the plaza. Abdul was still there and was being questioned by one of the officers. Everyone thought about stepping in, but nobody did. As Ramiro left, he heard someone throwing up in a corner.

Ramiro wouldn't know how to respond if someone asked him exactly why he had become an activist. All he knew was that hypocrisy was insupportable, and the city council wasn't doing much to deal with the misery he witnessed every day. He would repeat what he had heard so many times within the walls of the *okupa*: it was useless for the social democrats to tirelessly insist on the necessity of the tactical vote for the left, as after the elections 'the left' and 'the right' would implement practically exactly the same measures. Fascism had always been there, festering in the cement and the sewers of this alleged democratic state. The state was clear about who its enemies were, and PSOE – a party that was supposedly for the working-class socialists – was the state party *par excellence*.

As they demonstrated after the latest elections, PSOE preferred the corrupt right to govern rather than ceding to the timid reformism of Podemos on the left and the minimal concessions that the independentists asked for. They preferred to go to another vote rather than have a previously condemned social democratic party stick its nose in, a party that opposed the austerity measures dictated by Brussels and the European Union – read, lightly resisted, refused three times rather than zero, then allowed themselves to get fucked raw in the arse anyway. PSOE was, *de facto*, the party that had established Spain's economic model, starting with President Felipe González, his finance minister, Solchaga, and their first labour reforms, and then the introduction of precarity, the creation of IBEX 35, the privatisation of state monopolies, and President Zapatero's model of property market speculation and bank bailouts. PSOE had no qualms in continuing with the real estate policy strengthened by Aznar and his right-wing Partido Popular, nor in signing – along with the 'liberals' from the right – the reform of article 135 of the Constitution in order to guarantee debt payment priority.

Any party that played these games could only define themselves as a collaborator. The starry-eyed Podemos and their brilliant, lefty discourse just churned out the same old stories that had been heard so many times before. Nobody believed they were going to take the world by storm, or produce any genuine policies for the working class; nobody believed that anything that benefitted the working class could come from the capitalist state. Ramiro would tell everyone the same fable, that of SYRIZA and the Greeks, to prove that even in the sweetest of circumstances the results would be completely and utterly mediocre. Very well, very well. What happened with SYRIZA? They entered government with a landslide victory in 2015, showing up as the cool kids on motorbikes with a desire to stand up to the bad guys. They were there at Podemos' first party conferences. They said that they would open tough negotiations with the troika, that they would not put up with their contempt; they promised that Greece would not continue along the path of austerity; they said that they wouldn't allow a handful of rich countries from the north to piss in the mouths of the PIGS, of the 'piglets'. They called a referendum. Of course, it turned out that the people did not want austerity, how could they? But they ignored the people. They betrayed those who had voted for them, those who had seen a little bit of hope in them. They betrayed the people just like their comrades in the KKE, those good, keen-eyed Greek communists had said they would. The same crowd that just a few weeks earlier had gathered in Syntagma Square to support them with force, gathered once again, this time to see all their ministers hanged. VAT went up, they fucked over the retired by lowering pensions. They continued to call themselves the left, but they didn't recover from the shame they had brought down upon themselves; they condemned the future of a country forever, robbing the Greeks of the last thing they had, the slightest thing they clung on to: a little bit of hope.

What would the pseudo-lefties Podemos have done in their place? Well, nothing, stupid! All of this was simply the way of bourgeois parliamentarism, Ramiro would explain. The reformist detachments would continue to aspire to convince the communists that there was nothing contradictory about voting tactically in the elections, and then supporting the revolutionary movement for the rest of the year. They aspired to convince the communists that Podemos had a chance at governing Spain and transforming the world. But the communists' genuine task was to avoid the seizure of the popular movement to electioneering, to stop the carpet of bourgeois parliamentarism smothering the masses and their strength. Ramiro's task, in his eyes, was to prevent so many illusions being lost and so many hopes being wasted. His task was to unite rage to break everything.

Everyone knew that, despite claiming to be a left-wing party, Ahora Madrid would swallow, swallow, and continue to swallow the capitalist 'Operation Chamartín'. Everyone knew that Banco BBVA controlled the property developer Distrito Castellana Norte to a tune of more than 70%, and that the same bank monitored the expansion of the city by more than 70%, the result being that a whole sector of Madrid would be sold and privatised for the sole benefit of a bank. Everyone knew that they would sell this as a form of 'sustainable urbanisation', as the greenest form of development in all of history, that they'd continue selling and gentrifying it all, that they'd gentrify the working-class neighbourhood of Lavapiés (it was already on the verge) so they could build new hipster hotels. Everyone knew that this hypocrisy was insupportable and could only be met with revolution.

Many of the arguments that ran through Ramiro's over-stimulated mind appeared on the organisation's website that he oversaw. These ideas were also efficiently disseminated amongst the members so that they could repeat them in the different neighbourhood assemblies. *We cannot forget the moment our former mayor, leader of Ahora Madrid, Manuela Carmena, 'severed ties with all radical ideology to keep business owners quiet', as she affirmed with a happy smile, 'relax, I'm not a communist.'*

Ramiro repeated many things, but no one paid him much attention. Podemos had just won sixty-nine seats in the general elections. It was their third push, and they were just two steps away from becoming the majority party on the left. Ramiro insisted that the elections were subservient to the interests of the ruling class who controlled the mass media that formed public opinion, and throughout this frightening media spectacle, not one party questioned class oppression. He also called attention to how the Podemos leader, Pablo Iglesias, considered that 'small and medium businessmen were the people driving Spain forward', and not the proletariat.

Podemos, like someone who bragged and teased, *I know a song that will get on your nerves, get on your nerves, get get get on your nerves*, boasted of their sixty-nine seats, sixty-nine deputies, sixty-nine players, various city councils – Madrid included. They boasted of their sixty-nine human centipede parts and the shit that poured out of all their mouths. 'Whoever thinks they can end capitalism is naïve, and there's no naivety here,' said Pablo Iglesias on La Sexta Noche; the real gullible idiots were those who believed that Pablo Iglesias would end up being something other than the biggest cog in the bourgeois machine, the lackey that cranked the handle of capitalism, capable of kissing his flag and his ideology and his King and his patria. Ramiro insisted on all of this, trying so hard to believe himself, but he had friends who would just respond with sixty-nine seats and too many illusions.

Ramiro repeated that Manuela Carmena would lovingly plant one thousand little trees to hide what her Municipal Land and Housing Company was really doing, but none of it would go any further than aesthetics. The believers would respond with the argument that she was guaranteeing housing alternatives and creating a project that would make bin collections the responsibility of local councils. Ramiro would repeat that all of this would result in nothing, but those believers would argue that she was already pushing for change, and that Madrid would be completely and utterly transformed after a few years of her government and politics, enough to reverse the destruction caused by the Partido Popular.

One only needs to read a few pages of their manifesto, they would say. *A citizen audit of public debt, debt restructuring, the recovery of public management of currently outsourced local services, the elimination of seizures, subsidies and unjustifiable tax exemptions for private organisations, the creation of a public, regional-municipal bank, the visible identification of police officers, paralysation of forced terminations and evictions from first properties, application of the Historical Memory Law.* Ramiro tirelessly replied that none of this would happen, that Guillermo Zapata had already fallen from the city council, that so many more would fall, that soon there wouldn't be anyone remaining from the left, that death would come, and it would have the eyes of Manuela Carmena, it would be historic, and everything that remained would be left in the hands of PSOE, everything always remained for *the* PSOE, a party capable of converting neo Keynesian into a whorehouse tombola. He would ask them how they were so oblivious to the enormous scheme, the house of cards that was constructed to get their hopes up and play with their feelings, how they were so unaware that all these promises that they would walk the road to a freer, more beautiful and fairer world – a road without pain, without effort, without blood or tears – were empty.

Ramiro finally managed to sleep after a long while of staring at the ceiling, chewing his mind over with thoughts, thoughts about ideas, ideas about manifestos, manifestos about his dreams. He dreamt that the Partido Popular had built a huge dome over Madrid to isolate it from a timid socio-liberal government led by Pedro Sánchez and Alberto Rivera. Pollution meant that the air, no matter how many filters they installed, got trapped inside the asphyxiating dome, and an unofficial rule was enforced that recommended masks be worn within the perimeter of the city. Manuela Carmena was plugged into an artificial respiratory machine and the people from Ahora Madrid were waiting impatiently for her to wake up from the coma into which she had fallen after one of her councillors tweeted the innocent phrase 'expropriation of empty houses'. A woman who he could only see from the back praised traffic jams as a way of life and announced the privatisation of the health care system. The university hospital Ramón y Cajal would be sold to the owners of KFC Spain. He woke up suddenly after hearing former president José María Aznar's voice. Now, even more aged, moustache-less, with skeletal hands and skin so wrinkled that he resembled Palpatine in *Star Wars*, he declared that the Madrid government would last thousands and thousands and thousands of years...

In the morning he went to his Anthropology of Knowledges and Cultural Understanding class on the Somosaguas campus. Afterwards, he stopped by his house and then headed down a few streets to their base, where they had an important meeting. They had been urgently summoned to deal with kicking off a plan that had been on the back burner for a few months now. He still didn't know anything about it, but what they would decide there, in a room the size of a tiny bar, would change everything forever. Someone collected everyone's phones and took them away so that there could be no recording or spying – this wasn't an exceptional measure, but completely normal. The Central Committee presented their plan for the expropriation – the term officially used in order to establish a certain distance with respect to certain anarchist tendencies that fell under the terms *okupa* or squat – of the former Odeón studios. Ramiro had just found a purpose.

Launching flares at a mosque was not 'attacking' it but protesting in front of the building. Santiago didn't participate in the event, but he was present during the planning, and somebody had to compile the details of it all. The Spanish Network for Immigration and Refugee Aid would later come onto the scene as a private prosecutor: eleven accused of public disorder, the

Captain investigated. Santiago, the mere author of the photos but absent in all physical action, would be released: investigations rewarded those who were careful and erased their trail.

The smoke covered the entire bridge. He had imagined other things. He had painstakingly studied how many times Muslims prayed each day: five, they called it *salat*; they did not oblige themselves, rather subjected themselves to it without limits. *Faŷr, dhuhr, asr, magrib, isha*. He analysed their schedules and how long they took to clean themselves. He wondered if rituals were so different, or if it were only the actions taken by man that changed their meaning: word incarnated in the body, speech incarnated in substance, devotion through which the muscle and the bone and the flesh and the blood spoke. *Allahu akbar* indicated the start of the prayer.

He thought about one of their ideas that he had liked, *zakat*; the right of the poor and poverty-stricken, the obligation to give if you were above the *nisab*. It fascinated him that from the very beginning the Muslim religion had enforced tax. But the Galileans also distributed charity to their pagan brothers and sisters, and those who did not help the poor or less fortunate were not helped by God. The tight-fisted were present in all contexts. Of course, you had to take care of your own in order to purge oneself, keep one's hands clean, to be able to look others in the eyes without shame. Santiago would have also liked to see some churches burn: to dictate himself, following divine will, who entered heaven and who did not.

He gave free rein to the images, to the violence, a force that, once activated, did not stop: he photographed the white and red columns, the fire; he thought of disfigured faces, women burning beneath turbans, skin like the papyrus in Alexandria inflamed by dust and death. He would have thrown the fire inside the building and not in front of it: the final act in the protest seemed to him to be a symptom of cowardice. The many men he would have killed in order to preserve his purity accumulated on his conscience without weighing him down. Beyond the smoke from the flares, the light that gave shape to the world was filtering through the holes in the clouds.

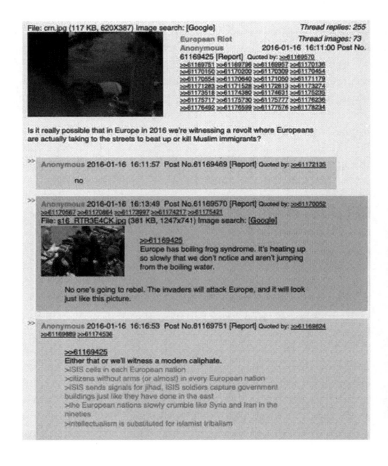

File: crn.jpg (117 KB, 620X387) Image search: [Google]   Thread replies: 255

European Riot   Thread images: 73
Anonymous   2016-01-16 16:11:00 Post No.
61169425 [Report] Quoted by: >>61169570
>>61169751 >>61169736 >>61169957 >>61170136
>>61170150 >>61170200 >>61170309 >>61170454
>>61170554 >>61170640 >>61171050 >>61171179
>>61171283 >>61171528 >>61172813 >>61173274
>>61173518 >>61174380 >>61174631 >>61175226
>>61175717 >>61175730 >>61175777 >>61176236
>>61176492 >>61176599 >>61177576 >>61178234

Is it really possible that in Europe in 2016 we're witnessing a revolt where Europeans are actually taking to the streets to beat up or kill Muslim immigrants?

Anonymous 2016-01-16 16:11:57 Post No.61169469 [Report] Quoted by: >>61172135

no

Anonymous 2016-01-16 16:13:49 Post No.61169570 [Report] Quoted by: >>61170052
>>61170667 >>61170864 >>61173997 >>61174217 >>61175421
File: s16_RTR3E4CK.jpg (361 KB, 1247x741) Image search: [Google]

>>61169425
Europe has boiling frog syndrome. It's heating up so slowly that we don't notice and aren't jumping from the boiling water.

No one's going to rebel. The invaders will attack Europe, and it will look just like this picture.

Anonymous 2016-01-16 16:16:53 Post No.61169751 [Report] Quoted by: >>61169824
>>61169989 >>61174536

>>61169425
Either that or we'll witness a modern caliphate.
>ISIS cells in each European nation
>citizens without arms (or almost) in every European nation
>ISIS sends signals for jihad, ISIS soldiers capture government buildings just like they have done in the east
>the European nations slowly crumble like Syria and Iran in the nineties
>intellectualism is substituted for islamist tribalism

The Brussels attacks had happened a day before they moved on the mosque. Nobody in the organisation had planned such an effort in just twenty-four hours. Borja had brought up the idea between beers on Three Kings night, when information about the wave of sexual assaults in Germany on New Year's Eve had started to circulate. They smoothed out the details and any rough edges in the days following. Then they waited for their first sign, the first excuse: the attack in Paris was too small to respond to with something so big and, not being one of theirs, the attacks in Iraq, Turkey, Indonesia, Burkina Faso, Somalia, Afghanistan, Pakistan, Egypt didn't matter enough for them to protest against them.

It wasn't easy to decide whether they were going to carry out the plan. Jesús, an eternal supporter of the Palestinian cause, thought that getting too caught up with the Arabs would distract them from the real issues, and that they – whilst so fanatical, so patriotic – were far from the worst. At each intervention, in an attempt to appear more intelligent, he would adjust his glasses and compulsively reposition his hair. He didn't take the slow, ideological transformations that took place in the Castillo well. Borja launched into a diatribe about the clash of civilisations, suggesting that in just a few years, if nobody tried to solve it, Europe would be nothing more than a new outfit of caliphates. They almost came to blows as, watching from the side-lines, Alejandro smirked without adding anything to the conversation. The Captain intervened before everything got out of hand.

'You really want to fight over this bullshit? Now? Now that we're preparing to take it further than we've ever taken it before? Jesús, you're right about one thing: we've always been anti-Zionist. We will never stop being so. But what threatens our race today – and remember, our race is our nation – is mass immigration, refugees, Islamists; that's what allows us to channel our rage, to destroy these ruins and build something else. The issue of contemporary liberal decadence has been eclipsed by this invasion, but soon there will be time to rebel against them too, cut off their ugly tentacles. Now the Islamists are knocking at the door, and we have to go down in history, not become history.'

Santiago saw Jesús' wry expression and guessed immediately at what he was thinking of saying. He took the opportunity, as they exchanged glances, to warn him with a subtle movement of his hand, decipherable as 'no fucking way, don't say it'. Mentioning the Captain's origins was out of the question.

'Alright, I get it. But are the Arabs, the Islamists really the problem? You know they aren't. Ask Borja, see if he understands who's behind the Great Replacement. Because I think he's confused.'

'Camus never said a thing about the Jews: what matters to us today is the giant influx of immigrants, refugees. The rest is nonsense,' Borja responded.

'Oh no? I guess he was talking about unicorns, yes, ha! Of course, your precious Camus was talking about unicorns when he said that every four in five employees at *France Culture* was Jewish, and that they even had at least one program a week to talk about Jews. And of course, he was also talking about unicorns when he insinuated that *that* culture could be whatever it wanted, but not French. And that it was called, and is called, overrepresentation. We can't say anything, because they'd call us antisemites. But you know that, of course. But they were overrepresented for a reason. Each one of them, occupying a French employee's space, substituting the voice of a French man or woman. That's what he said. But no, ok, your dear Renaud Camus never said anything about the Jews.'

The conversation bored the others present to death as they couldn't care less about what that freak Camus said or not – *wasn't he the Nobel guy?* one of them asked. The root of their indifference was sociological, well studied: ever since it had been founded two years earlier, the Castillo had been made up of a rather eclectic group of people, and these guys' interests were founded in the movement of the football hooligans from Real Madrid and Atletico. Those guys didn't give a shit about that 'French philosophy nonsense'. No, the skinheads were simply present at the spectacle that some of them politely nicknamed 'debate club' others, 'the nerd-orgy' – these guys would argue over spilt milk before they decided whether they were going to graffiti some random thing on the side of a building or not. Santiago didn't take to the floor so much, at least not in public, and almost never in the after-dinner conversation, but he belonged, without a doubt, to the 'the nerd-orgy' sub-group. He despised dick heads more than he despised scholars, and he preferred by far that his discussions were with people prone to reading and not with those built like brick shithouses.

The Captain leaned back in her chair and stretched her arms out until her hands reached the shelves behind her. She didn't grab a book, but rather something that almost looked like a trashy novella, a fanzine leaflet. She quickly flicked through the pages and the group waited in silence until she started to read.

'The French State, through its policies, its laws, and its courts, organised "the Great Replacement" of populations by imposing preference for immigrants and Islamists, with more than eight million Arab Muslims (and counting), bringing another history, another civilisation, and another future to the country: sharia. The French State has long been set on being a part of the rupturing of our national tradition. See the 14th of July: it celebrates a disgusting revolt and not the grandiosity of unity. See the ridiculous emblem of the French Republic: a plaster-cast Marianne with a revolutionary Phrygian hat. See the atrocious logos that they have imposed to replace the coats of arms for the traditional regions. Remember that in 1962, the State deployed all its force against the Algerian French, abandoning them to their fate.'

'So nothing about Jews.'

The Captain sighed. 'Leave the Jews out of it for a bit. Yeah, yeah, we all know about the Kalergi Plan. But do you think we'd seem like nice guys if we said, I don't know, that it was the Jews' fault? Do you think that anyone would believe us anymore, have more faith in us if we focused on that rather than speaking about solidarity and social justice for the Spanish? Really, Jesús, do you really think the problem right now is the Jews? Our people, here, dying of hunger, and all the aid is going elsewhere. It's unacceptable. That's what we truly believe in, that's our moral commitment. All the rest is filament, muscles, arteries. If you allow me, love for our own kind is the heart.'

'I haven't forgotten that Gaza is the biggest concentration camp in the world. Have you?'

'Don't piss me off.'

The atmosphere soured whenever any of the Captain's old friends – activists that she had dragged with her when she was putting together the Castillo – boldly seconded Jesús' words. Santiago was very thankful for what came next, which was a ceasefire of almost divine intervention similar to the ones that armies lived through on equally festive dates: the Captain's son, about three years old, had woken up and requested his mother's company and so she immediately left the room and suggested to the others that they started to get their stuff together, the homeless that they put up there would also be wanting to sleep. They obeyed.

Santiago grabbed his backpack, picked up his belongings, slipped on his coat and didn't stick around to chat with the others as they chained up the red gates and made suggestions about heading to a bar in the area. He walked down towards

Paseo Castellana where he got on the night bus in front of the Ministry of the Interior. Waiting in disgust for the racket on the bus to stop, he ignored the men squaring up to one and other and turned up his music before getting off in Puente de Vallecas and making his way to Calle Pico Cejo. He didn't make eye contact with anyone he passed, he didn't nod his head towards beggars, he didn't feign a mutual understanding, he didn't grimace with disapproval. When he got back his father still wasn't home. He wanted to listen at the window for the infernal noise of a bin lorry, like a rocket taking off, and try to identify if it was him; he wanted, for a second, that the stench lifted and circulated the flat, flooded into the nooks and crannies, he wanted to smell that foul stink, to shut it in, close all the doors and windows. He slung his backpack into the depths of his bedroom. He programmed some tweets from the organisation's official account for the coming days.

It was a night like so many others. He never normally went out. He had spent the whole week following the incidents in Cologne, refreshing /pol/, a forum on 4chan, a hegemonic image board or crazy box full of anonymous people capable of shouting at the same time. /pol/, in short, stood for Politically Incorrect, a floodgate that filtered the discussions about world events and political matters so they didn't drown out the rest of the more or less peaceful sections.

He couldn't sleep, so he logged on with the rest of the forum users – at this hour, mostly north American – and obsessively searched for any images of the sexual assaults. He hoped some had emerged, not out of morbidity, but to feed his already present hatred; he wanted to gather more corrosive acid, fuel-up, prepare himself. He found other images that didn't satisfy his impulses at all in the same way, but he was incapable of letting it go. He left /pol/, went over to the Wikipedia page and refreshed it again and again to see if there was more information. The final number of criminals increased adequately. After a while, a long time after he had stopped consulting the page, the number passed two thousand, and months later, in July, the Federal Office of Criminal Investigation confirmed that one thousand two hundred women had been sexually assaulted that night.

Sexual assaults on New Year's Eve in Germany	
Place	Cologne (principally), Berlin, Bielefeld, Düsseldorf, Frankfurt, Hamburg and Stuttgart, Germany
Coordinates	50°56'32"N 6°57'28"E
Target(s)	Young women
Date	31st December 2015 and 1st January 2016
Type of attack	Sexual assault, rape, and mugging
Injured	At least 2 rapes and more than 200 sexual assaults and muggings (in Cologne)
Perpetrator(s)	At least 31
Suspect(s)	More than 1000 males of Arabic and North African origin

[edit data on Wikidata]

During New Year's Eve celebrations on the 31st of December 2015, a wave of collective sexual assaults, robberies, muggings, and at least two cases of rape, all against women, took place in Germany, for the most part in Cologne, but also in Finland, Sweden, Switzerland, and Austria. In Germany, this wave of crime affected twelve cities: Frankfurt, Hamburg, Stuttgart, Bielefeld, Düsseldorf and more. In the city of Cologne alone, the number of aggressors was estimated to be around 1,500. The attacks were coordinated and carried out by groups of between two and forty men, all described as North-African or Arab. The suspects were mostly asylum seekers or illegal immigrants. In Cologne, the number of incidents reported continued to rise each day: 30 were reported on the 4th of January, 516 on the 10th of January, and 560 on the 11th of January – 40% of these reported rape or sexual assault. The number of reports rose to 652 on the 14th of January, of which 50% reported sexual assault. In Arabic countries this phenomenon is known as 'taharrush gamea': 'collective sexual harassment'.

The silence of the police and the media, their leniency, the declarations made by the mayor of Cologne who blamed German women, and the tardiness with which the media (above all public channels) reported the aggressions, was strongly criticised.

Heiko Maas, the German Minister of Justice, stated, 'when a gang like this gets together to break the law, the action appears to be, in some way or another, organised action. Nobody could make me believe that this was not planned or prepared.'

'We are beginning to suspect that behind these very organised aggressions that many women suffered across multiple German cities on the night of New Year's Eve, lies Islamic terrorism's new strategy for destabilisation.'

For several days the sexual assaults were not mentioned on any form of mainstream German media. As a result, the German media suffered an explosion of criticism that they are still facing *today, and the media and the police force were accused of having ignored or camouflaged the facts, for fear that they could incite criticisms of the German government during the migration crisis. On the 5th of January, the television channel ZDF made a statement of apology, admitting they had made 'a clear error regarding the facts.' The attacks did not appear in the French press until the 6th of January.*

Investigating the delay in information on the part of police authorities in Cologne, the media revealed that the communications from the directors of the police force contradicted the declarations made by police officers in situ. *In an interview with a high-up civil servant in the police force, the newspaper* Bild *unveiled that the authorities received strict instructions from their superiors to not inform journalists of the infractions committed by refugees. These confessions reinforced the German population's discontent regarding the coverage of the migration crisis, judging it insufficient.*

Conservative sociologist and critic of multiculturalism, Mathieu Bock-Côté, interpreted the voluntary silence of the media as 'one more piece of evidence of the media-politics complex that filters ideologically bad news that could compromise, in one way or another their myth of a peaceful, multicultural coexistence.'

An important fact to consider when interpreting the outrage seen in Germany following the aggressions, is Cologne's symbolic aspect. The city is home to a cathedral constructed six-hundred years ago, a building that withstood constant air raids during the Second World War, making it one of the most visited monuments in Germany. To make matters worse, German train stations are usually considered by its citizens as safe places.

Germany, and particularly Cologne, has had many experiences with mass protests such as the Love Parade, *fan zones in Berlin, and the enormous popular festivals organised in regional capitals. Cologne is one of the most liberal and cosmopolitan German cities, with a diverse and solid society. These elements point to the symbolic collapse that citizens experienced before these mass aggressions.*

In addition, Germany was a country in which very few women experienced public aggressions. Thus, these crimes are completely new to German men and women.

Surveys carried out within the migrant population show immense cultural divergences. For example, more than 90% of Tunisians and Moroccans believe that women should always obey their husband.*

The composition of the page annoyed him: it sounded like a text that was far too amateur, something that could be ripped apart at the seams at the first intervention of moderators. The rhetoric, whilst its sources were reliable, sounded like nothing more than a mediocre essay written by a GCSE student. He didn't change anything: he waited to see how long it would last like that. Years later, it surprised him to see that the reference to Mathieu Bock-Côté had not only resisted the passage of time and sedimentation, but had also been expanded upon: in 2021, the page also criticised some declarations made by the journalist Brice Couturier, a fervent Macronist, according to whom, 'the willingness to conceal the events in Cologne was a danger to democracy and a breach of commitment to the social contract.' 'When a State, in the name of an ideology that is seen as unpopular, such as multiculturalism, refuses to guarantee the free movement of women in public spaces and attempts to dissuade them from filing reports, the social contract is threatened.'

The statistic about 90% of Tunisians and Moroccans was also still there in 2021, strengthened with a link to *The Economist*. Declarations about how in Germany, 'very few women experienced public aggressions', only emphasised the unusualness – or the paradigm, to be ostentatious, resonant, flowery – of the

---

* Translator's own translation from the Wikipedia page, 'Sexual Aggressions on New Year's Eve in Germany', from the 16th of January 2016, French version.

crimes. There was only a slight modification in the wording, changed in order to convert the text into a hypothesis of a 'historical' nature. The entire paragraph on the symbolism of Cologne, which seemed to him like an utter discursive mediocrity, remained intact in 2021.

> Anonymous 2016-01-16 17:59:55 Post No.61176321 [Report]
>
> I would love for there to be an enormous Islamist terrorist attack here in Amsterdam, Wilders would rise in less than a day and protests would explode everywhere. Only then could you justify the assassination of so much greasy rubbish, of shit-coloured races, and return our country to the white territory it should never have stopped being.

He returned to /pol/ and couldn't contain himself: he burst out into laughter and quickly covered his mouth for fear of annoying the neighbours. He realised how insane his behaviour was. He stopped. He closed the page, logged off, thought about how crazy they all were, the bedlam that surrounded the organisation, the idiots and dimwits that practically all its members were. For Juanma, a bumbling idiot, he only had words of disapproval. Jesús was obsessed with the Jews but hid the fact that his third surname was Peralta. And Alejandro, always accompanied by his henchmen, was a brute. Santiago's companions looked like a disagreeable joke compared to the sophistication of the trolling he saw in other parts. They were mere caricatures, and un-funny ones at that; they were frustrated specimens who poured their rage into nocturnal punch-ups and beating up immigrants and gays after a few nights of beer and Charlie, beer and Charlie, beer and Charlie until they were almost dead. They never consumed anything within the Castillo, they always did that stuff far from the building: *officially*, the consummation of drugs, alcohol, or any other substances was not permitted on the premises. Some nights there was beer, but it was sworn and perjured that there was to be nothing more. Santiago almost never went out with them, and he was sure that that rose suspicions: he was certain that if he hadn't been a activist for such a long time, they'd think he had infiltrated the group, that he was a spy. However, not only did he have the Captain's absolute confidence, but along with her, he had been the principal ideologist of this whole process of *de-demonisation.* They never spoke, like those hot-heated forum goers, of greasy rubbish, shit-coloured races, latinos, moors, faggots, AIDS carriers, fags, trannys, paedos, Indians, junkies, or jewish pigs: the focus had to be absolutely on the fact, on us, on us against them, on the people, on those at the bottom, on the patriots. They almost never spoke of identity; the objective was always to reach the Spanish (they did so by mentioning the word *España* a lot). Their aim was social justice for Spanish citizens, glory for their nation. Being Spanish was not only about blood, but many other things that had always been and always would be obvious. They got rid of all the old-smelling symbology and instilled a feeling in the hearts of men that was similar to danger. They stuck with that which awakened emotions, inspired love, rage, or passion. They demonised the enemy: those who didn't want them to provide a roof over the heads of those who had nothing, or didn't support this act. This was an enemy that came to harm them, an enemy against whom they had to defend themselves, because the Castillo was peaceful and made sacrifices, they worked hard, they were committed. If they wanted to let it slip that their nation was becoming substituted for another, that of the immigrants, they would let it slip, but they didn't dwell on it. What they insisted on was how disgraceful it was that they were given a roof, a shelter, and a life whilst the Spanish were abandoned. Because the truth was that today, the Spaniard was poor, even if they were supportive of the miseries suffered by those from outside. Closing the door of your house to protect your own was not being mean towards those who knocked at it. The organisation conveyed the rage, the discontentment, the misery. They were the voice of the abandoned, the voice of those without a voice, they offered a roof to those who did not have a roof, gave arms to those who did not have arms, gave a flag to those who felt abandoned by the State, made them believe in a future, made them believe that they were not eternally trapped in the past; they allowed men to feel they were the heirs of a legendary race, from a long lineage that ended with them, and would only continue through their sons who would give shape to the world when their turn came, and would continue to do so until the end of time. The plan could not have been going more smoothly: it was working exactly how sincerity that came from the heart worked; it was moving forwards far better than brutish, unthoughtful ideologies would. They transmitted ideas as if they were performing a blood transfusion, as if there were no difference between the one speaking and the one being spoken to. Santiago was untouchable, he was the Captain's right hand man, the great father of the theories that backed up all she was constructing. She knew he didn't get involved in the trouble, that he would always be there, that he only aspired to reap what he sowed.

Santiago continued to hope, day and night, day and night. And then something happened – between his hands, on his phone screen – that he would prefer was omitted from this story, and the story obeys.

PART TWO:
GREED

Sometimes cities are built on whims. In Madrid there was a world that existed apart from the rest: AZCA, the financial district found on the Avenida del Generalísimo. Franco was dead, but of course it was already too late to change acronyms, redistribute names, pass the dominance that some lorded over the lives of others from one hand to another. Near the Avenida del Generalísimo was the enormous Torre Windsor, famous, above all, for its destruction: things known for their collapse always tend to be the most idealised. A random woman who was working in the offices – it could have been anyone, she could have been substituted for any other person – confirmed before a judge that she had indeed smoked a couple of cigarettes at work, something that wasn't considered a sufficient cause for an entire building to burn down in such a way. As such, more speculations arose: a mysterious stranger spotted in the photo-copy room, a random hole that had appeared in the garage that someone had snuck in through, padlocks that had been forced open, secret doors, passageways between buildings, private documents from the Ministry of Defence and state secrets hidden in briefcases; anything, including ghosts, was capable of infesting Madrid like a parasite, swelling its arteries with cement and burning in the air. None of these speculations bore fruit. The fire went out but started to burn again. After just a few years, its mere mention was capable of ageing any text. Because soon after this we learned of the fires in the Santo Tomás church, the Quinta de la Esperanza church, the Ministry of War, and the Ribera de Curtidores. We knew with absolute certainty what the mistakes were that caused a brutal gas explosion on Calle Toldeo, we also knew the names of so many monks and dead residents who by now had long been resting in God's bosom, drugged by methane or put to sleep by electric shocks, but we would remain ignorant to the why behind the revived incandescence of the Torre Windsor fire. Beyond knowing the name of the person who wanted to see everything burn, the person that benefitted from the disaster, we knew nothing. The building's fall, supposedly the work of one José Manuel Villarejo, saw the disappearance of documents that allegedly linked the president of Banco BBVA from 2000-2018, Don Francisco González Rodríguez, with an auditor from Deloitte who was – according to *El País* – allegedly summoned 'by the Anti-corruption Prosecutor's Office the day before the catastrophe'. Don Julián Reyzábel, owner of Torre Windsor and a real estate mogul, an architect of the world, the demiurge of self-made Spains, built vulgar constructions where before only a Manchego *pueblo* existed. He converted Madrid into the perfect playground for mischief, lewdness, and venom: he was the owner of Calle de la Montera, University Carlos III, the Palacio de la Prensa, Plaza del Callao, the Ciudad Lineal district, Calle Bristol, Calle París, the Roxy Cinema, the Consulate, Calle Bilbao, the Canciller cinema, the Versalles Hotel and the Victoria Theatre. He brought entire generations closer to rancidity and life, he created a very *typical Spanish way of life* that was populated with pleasure, naked bodies, cocks, and tits. He also fancied himself a producer, and had the directors Fernando Esteso and Andrés Pajares wrapped around his little finger: he invented his own cinema that was a faculty of suggestion, the impossible, an attempt at imagination. If we were going to be picky, we could go so far as to say that Julián Reyzábal invented a way of pleasing himself that didn't exist until he made it, a brand-new self-pleasure company in which no one had to drop their hands. The patriarch died in 1978, with an eternal image of Torre Windsor still branded on his retinas, no possibility of flames, fires, or controlled demolition existed in his eyes.

Plagues of money spread from one limb to another, creating diseased or gangrenous extremities that no one was kind enough to amputate: the plague raged until flies and ants came to eat tongues, and cockroaches that chewed eardrums as if they were chewing gum crawled out of ears. Money corrupted, money was a hell strangled in ivy and mother of pearl, a hell covered in corpses. Reyzábal's youngest son died in December of 2011 at seventy-eight years old, having received the holy sacraments under the mantle of the Virgin Pilar. His funeral took place on the 9th of the month, at 7pm in the Parish Church of Santa María de Caná de Pozuelo de Alarcón. The children distributed the many responsibilities he left behind between them. One – accused of abuse, his sentence appealed nine times and finally acquitted in a case in which the judge called the accusing party a 'brat' and a 'bitch' – was appointed director of several companies and managing director of the real estate company Seiga. Together, the heirs continued to run a variable capital investment company with a maximum statutory capital of twenty-four million euros. They named one of the cousins chief executive officer in several of the businesses, and also gave the cousin's brother something, given that their aunt had previously held various positions in the empire. They also continued with the work of Reyza 2006, a real estate company with more than one hundred million euros of share capital. Another one of the children became the directing manager of Abraxas, a fund with interest in photovoltaic energy, and they built and constructed and built and constructed with the New Winds Group. They continued their work in the Nueva Najarra and Espectáculos Callo production companies, thanks to which they controlled the most important cinemas in Madrid – it was almost like public pro bono: someone had to keep the culture alive, and it wouldn't be the city council. Imagine a family that controlled where you lived, what you smelled like, how you turned on the lights, what you saw, what you thought, what you listened to, the reason you got fired, your free time, your slavery, your eviction, your alcohol consumption, your drug consumption, your future prospects. The extermination of the social class to which they did not belong was on the mind of every good *madrileño*, unless, of course, they benefitted from their antagonist's productive forces, or thrived thanks to the power that was brought on by resentment. There were several families like this, capable of writing History – with a capital H – without ever touching a book, imagining a narrative, or putting black ink to white paper. These were families that had given shape to cities, cities that they always had a quantifiable, measurable percentage of, knowing at just a glance exactly how much of the territory they observed could belong to them; they speculated with resources on what they even – shamelessly – came to call *futures*. In a long, historical process, the ability of these groups of individuals to transform the world exceeded that of kings, the nobility, and ancient aristocracies. Today, power was distributed in more perverse relationships, articulated in the phrase 'public-private collaboration'. And power was inherited. Can we blame poor Reyzábal, that shabby old man, the first man among men, for having had a good idea and laying the first stone, for having made contacts, for having yearned for everything? He was born in the countryside in the village of Caleruega. He built summer cinemas, the ones that everyone loved so much; then he wanted to buy cinemas and sites, and cinemas and sites, and cinemas and sites until there was no waste ground left in Madrid. Were there not alternatives with less nobility? There were those who built their fortune on broken hands and then retired far from civilisation and its dead, making donations to wash their bad consciences: Reyzábal only wanted the great cage of the world to resemble his mind, he only wanted the city in which he landed to be made in his image and likeness. He was not a dirty bourgeois heir to the slave trade, as he might have been; he did not make his fortune by throwing dirt on top of those repressed by the regime, as so many others like him would have done. He did not build our cultural institutions whilst honouring financiers of the 1936 coup d'état, as some did. If we compared Reyzábal to the others, his was a story with very little blood: an excessive, but well-distributed, fortune; a wealth built without the dead having to sacrifice themselves over and over again. But! Should we consider him *legitimate*? Should we believe that just because he did not keep corpses in his closet that this implied he did not continue to produce them? Madrid, if it were to consider its subjects, would determine that it was convenient for their imagination to be pious: but it also had to consider that this desire for something more, to want to have or to be something else, was actually quite ubiquitous, almost omnipresent, because the city itself imprinted it on the bodies that it chewed up and spat out.

The building that was formerly home to the Odeón studios, located on Calle de la Encomienda, was Reyzábal family property through Nueva Cosica, the limited company that had a net income of almost twenty-million euros in 2014.

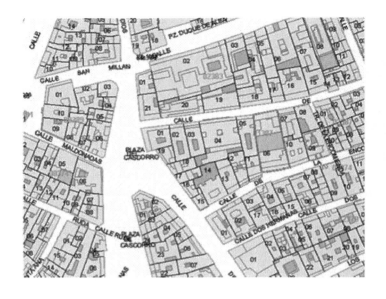

They had amplified coordination efforts with the neighbours and comrades from other occupied buildings in the vicinity and Madrid in general. After they had analysed the position of the building, everyone became well aware that they wouldn't be able to enter, let alone stay there, if they didn't put together a coordinated action plan that covered even the finest of details. They issued the announcement over a few days: they would organise a big festival with a parade and a solidarity street market along the building's street and in the surrounding areas. Promoted by several other organisations, the festival would include drum circles, a brass band, dance groups, performances, activist art, jazz, swing, food stands with acheke, debates about networks, raids, power and potency, and the touristification of the neighbourhood and the centre of Madrid, as well as the collection of funds for neighbourhood celebrations in Lavapiés. It would begin at five in the afternoon, with the idea being that it would continue until whenever was necessary; nobody put up any obstacles.

They set up the food stands and carefully hung the banners and garlands in such a way that they concealed the entrance to their objective. The other day, José brought up one of the most complicated questions regarding the 'expropriation': the owners, while they had not installed alarms or security cameras, would surely know that a building of that size in such an a turbulent area was a tempting prize. These were, according to the narrative perpetuated by the media, the glory years for *okupas*, squats and drug dens, situations that were 'proliferating' in entire cities, transforming neighbourhoods in Madrid, Barcelona, and other regional capitals into authentic pits of terror. Little old grannies no longer knew what they were going to find when they stepped out of their home and onto the street: perhaps they would bump into some poor homeless guy cutting three lines of whatever substance on a window ledge, the Iberian Peninsula becoming the next Sacred Fentanyl Empire. The mainstream media had started to alternate – following the formats learned by screenwriters in international academies – between conspiracy A, sub-conspiracy B, and finally sub-conspiracy C, the first occupying triple the amount of airtime than the third, and the second, twice as much. Conspiracy A described, with finesse, the nasty existence of squatters, warning old ladies of lefty, disorderly Podemos or Candidatura d'Unitat Popular supporting youth who were ready to enter their apartments and change the locks as soon as they popped out to buy bread. They explained, in fact, that the leader of Podemos, Pablo Iglesias – if he ever got to govern – would establish a constitutional law that would give squatters the moral rights to claim control of a building if the grandma who lived in it was absent for whatever reason, because Pablo would bring morality into what was administered by law. Sub-conspiracy B focused on drug-dens, 'drug supermarkets', el Raval and the hellish Sant Antoni in Barcelona, the syringes in Lavapiés, and the questionable comings and goings in Puente de Vallecas; it conspired that the mayoresses of Madrid and Barcelona, the evil stepsisters Carmena and Colau, were plotting together. Sub-conspiracy C homed in on the announcements made by security companies, and their insistency, first and foremost on private alarms and surveillance, cameras, and control, and secondly, on the possibility of recovering occupied housing though force, in the style of paramilitary brigades, thanks to companies like Un-occupy, made up of militiamen from Eastern Europe, mixed martial arts fighters, and business men who funded groups from the extreme right. But let's rewind: landlords would never install security cameras, it would be too expensive and would give them little return. (God only knew that one of the principal characteristics of the rich was that they were tight fisted, which is exactly why they never made it to heaven.) No, instead they blocked off the entrance to a building by placing a ropey, precariously laid brick wall behind the first flimsy shutter. It was a huge relief to find that there was not a camera system in the Odeón building; though discovering that there wasn't an accessible entrance either was a minor inconvenience. After a couple of weeks, Ramiro would later come to hear that they had been toying with the idea of entering the building via the roof, with the help of some neighbours who lived in a nearby attic. However, they had eventually chickened out, having decided that it would have all been too exposed, too obvious. Instead, Carlos and Luis, who were in charge of the operation, now took care of forcing open the padlock on the metal shutters so they could remove it. They first attempted it with a crowbar but had no luck, so asked those who were stood outside on the street to turn up the music so they could get out the drill. It gave way easily and they quickly got out all the tools they needed to replace the expired padlock; they widened the holes so they could twist in some thicker screws, fixed on the new padlock, and locked it shut. Following the others' orders, Luis left, making it look as if he were picking up beer and food for the stalls. Then, a second group snuck behind the canvases and banners with maces and mallets: they started to pick away at the temporary brick wall behind the shutter, taking advantage of the beats of the drum circle to hit in time with the rhythm, or listening out for when the music from the performances was louder. Courteously, they stopped when a collaborator told them a neighbour was complaining of the noise, and they all breathed a simultaneous sigh of relief when it turned out that the source of the complaint was the noise being made by the Pachanga music. A third division coming out of a nearby apartment brought supports and metal sheets to prepare what would be, after the padlocked shutter, the building's new, second protective layer. They finally succeeded in picking a small hole in the wall through which the first person could pass, but it was not yet sizeable enough for them to enter with everything they needed. Vera was the first to go through with a first-aid kit, the banner, water, and some plastic bags in her backpack. Ramiro followed with little more than a torch, his phone, and his laptop. The others would stay back to continue chipping away at the bricks.

The door to the building's foyer was immediately on their left as they entered through the hole. Ramiro turned on his torch. They had made it into the studio's former foyer. It was completely empty but still intact. One wall was lined in plasterboard and coated in a black checked finish that reflected the light. The others were yellow with blue skirting and doors; the floor was tiled. There were several small adjoining rooms that were all completely empty, and some hallways. They advanced a little towards an atrium with black stippled walls in which the ruins of an old stage persisted. They explored the interior galleries before coming up against a wall. Their eyes focused, first of all, on the sound proofing panels, then on the enormous dark blue curtain. They tried to open the emergency exits but found them walled up. Upon seeing the ceiling spotlights, they wasted no time in finding the switchboard, though their attempts to get it working were fruitless. Ramiro sent a message to the group to warn them: we're going to have to wire the electricity. Every source of natural light had been bricked up. Vero stopped to marvel at the blue canvas and asked Ramiro if he had thought about the sort of things they'd filmed here. He wouldn't have heard her were it not for the echo, which startled him: the sound amplified and filled the whole building, it almost reverberated from one wall to the other, ignoring the forces that were put in place to control it, forces that in another time an interior designer had carefully planned. He realised that they had been silent up to this point, and he couldn't accept that the silence had been broken. He responded, avoiding the question: in that moment he couldn't imagine anything, let alone who had walked these floors before him, or who had dirtied their hands building it. He turned back and walked up some stairs, upon which he found a dead rat. He held in his scream. Vero took charge of putting it in a bag and they continued up the stairs together, walked through a door, and reached the old projection room. It had been modernised, but Ramiro knew that it was at least one hundred years old. He looked for the projector but found nothing. They had planned to put some money together to buy one: they were already thinking ahead. He went on taking pictures of every new room, asking Vero to hold the torch and light up specific corners. They sat down on the steps for a moment, paying close attention to the numbered stairs, their gazes drawn to the wall that was home to the screen; it was talismanic, mystical. He felt like they had won the lottery, they were going to do big things here. Overwhelmed, he then began to think about everything they would have to reconstruct within the ruins. It was only in his final, fleeting thoughts that he imagined all the faces to whom a place like this could give shelter, and he was ashamed to have put himself first, ashamed of believing that the Odeón studios were waiting for only him. He was embarrassed by the image that came to him of himself surrounded by books. It was like a crappy still from a film in 68', the wall behind him painted blue and white, covered in slogans penned in black, the whiteboards for José's classes nearby. He took a while to snap out of his trance. Vero was nudging him.

'Are you listening to me? Come on, we've gotta get a fucking move on.'

They found more rooms. A poster for *Átame*: Victoria Abril, Antonio Banderas, an Almodóvar production. He went up to the rooftop and was blinded upon opening the trapdoor. Until now, he hadn't noticed the sheer amount of dust that was inside the building, the weight of the atmosphere, the damp, the stench of pestilence, abandonment, and neglect. He flung his backpack onto the roof and breathed, once, twice; he took sharp, quick breaths, trying to concentrate on the inhales and exhales. He felt a pinch of anxiety in his chest and his head felt like it was on the brink of imploding. He leaped on his backpack, rummaged around for a pill, swallowed it without water and fell to the floor. Mouth open, arms wide, he lay there like a star observing the travelling clouds. He heard Vero's voice asking him if he was ok, he responded with a yes. Vero told him that some of the others had already joined them inside and they were going to continue with the reconnaissance mission. No rush. Ramiro slowly sat himself up without lifting his body too much in order to avoid being seen, and saw that Calle de la Encomienda was a celebration of colours that stretched all the way down the street right up to Plaza Cascorro; it was a huge festival, a great cry of joy and light. A couple danced, parting and coming back together, allowing themselves to spin back into each other's arms. Curious passers-by approached to see what was happening and ended up staying, a little less in love with themselves, a little more in love with what was happening around them. From here, he could see San Andrés church and, a little further away, the horror that was the Almudena cathedral. He saw every open, circular courtyard, corral like, the interaction between neighbours, the clothes lines strung between one extreme and the other like an invitation to tightrope walkers. He suddenly felt like he was being watched and he ducked down, returning to the shadows. He was absolutely sure someone was watching him, he knew with scientific certainty that another person had been close by, watching him crouched and in waiting like a predator and he felt ashamed, not because the other person had been the predator, but because he was. He didn't want to look back out. He rejected the sun, turned his back to the clouds and started heading down the stairs, slamming the trapdoor shut behind him. He convinced himself that he had been daydreaming, that no one had really been there, and he reminded himself that there had been no whistle-blowers: he couldn't ruin the entire mission, he wasn't going to be the one that ruined everything. He promised himself he wouldn't share his paranoia with anybody. He found the rest of them. He hugged Quique and picked up a broom and began to sweep without thinking, and Quique asked him what the fuck he was doing and told him there would be time for that later, passing him a sandwich.

They provisionally settled themselves in the projection room. Quique and Luis had brought more food and some sleeping bags. José stood up and began to speak.

'I suppose you might have been told that there's an initial period of 48 hours, from which point on we're safe and they can no longer kick us out. Get that out of your heads; forget it. It supposedly comes from precedent, but in criminal law, precedent never means rights; they can kick us out of here whenever they want. Our strategy is different. First: we set ourselves up, clean, reclaim the building, and get to know the neighbours. It's key that we get on their good side and can be absolutely sure that none of them are going to turn on us and report us. It would be great if they can't link the festival we've organised with the occupation, but that's secondary: there are too many organisations implicated in the festival for that to matter, having so many people involved plays in our favour. The building's not used as housing, so the whole thing is less urgent for them. But for us, yes, it's urgent: in fact, the supposed crime we are committing, like you might have heard before, still calls what we are doing home invasion. Ramiro has the all the communications ready to post on social media, and the photos he's taken are for exactly that. It doesn't matter so much, the police are going to come all the same, and they'll try to intimidate us, but they're not going to get in… and they have to believe that we've been here a while. Just in case they connect the dots, we'll publish everything online the day after tomorrow.'

'And then?' asked Vero.

'We anticipate and summon, through social media and sending out messages, the entirety of the city of Madrid and its suburbs, we hope that the people come out and support us until the pigs have no choice but to leave. Of course, they'll think up more strategies, but at the start we have to make sure we apply more than enough pressure. I'm not saying it's going to be piss easy, evidently, but let's see.'

Now it was Quique's turn.

'If you're here, it's because you're committed. Many more of us will join in the days to come but, for now, at the beginning, we need people who have the time to assure permanence. Tonight, we'll wire the electricity; if we're lucky everything will work, and we'll have light. You live further away Vero, and it makes sense for you to stay here anyway. Ramiro, if you can, because you live nearby, bring books or something, anything that will make the nights a bit easier. Right now, it's not the most welcoming atmosphere, and we're going to be shut in here for a good while. The best thing is that no one sees too much movement, and that the movement that is seen is as controlled as possible, we want to catch them by surprise. This place was completely abandoned, and for now there's no renovation project planned, so no one's going to come by until the police or the landlord arrive, if they feel like it.'

'And no one suspects a thing?' asked Vero.

'At the moment, they're too worried that the festival's going to turn into a big piss-up. If they do suspect anything, we're fucked: the closest pig is walking around less than five-hundred metres away from us.'

The central courtyard in the Castillo was full, like every Sunday. Everyone formed little huddles to chat, ask how the week had gone, or share the cigarettes that from time to time they begged off the members. There were mothers – just mothers – who came with their children, dirty hair, and grime under their finger-nails; they grouped together to better endure the cold and let their kids run around. He couldn't deny it, Santiago was proud of the Sundays and all the children that they were managing to give a better life, or even just a bit of dignity – he almost considered it his great social project. The idea wasn't entirely his (it was, in fact, a complete carbon copy), but he had set it in motion, pushed it, resolved. He coordinated the paperwork that oversaw how many packages of non-perishable food would go to each family per week, he read and re-read their records attentively. Along with the Captain he prepared outlines of the groups of activists within the Castillo, among which they then distributed various tasks and placed at strategic points during the three weekly collections that nourished the food bank. He had also come up with the idea that the people benefitting from the Castillo's efforts should meet certain requirements. These requirements were never considered a strict criterion, as then it would have been impossible for them to have access to aid, but rather a defence mechanism, a measure that would make any boycott attempt almost impossible. The families interested in the food bank, just like those who were considered socially excluded and used the facilities in the Castillo, had to, by protocol, go through an interview stage in which either himself or the Captain was present. As for those who resided in the Castillo, it meant that none were infiltrators; for the hungry, it was purely a question of dissuasiveness. The Castillo was in the north of the city, relatively far from the colossal nuclei of *madrileño* poverty, but people still came to them from those southern neighbourhoods like Carabanchel and Vallecas, as well as from Tetuán in the North. Their intake was extremely controlled: they had to avoid the constant threat of the antifascists. Those looking for help would arrive at the Castillo mumbling quietly, with an incorrectly paid metro ticket, following a recommendation from another outcast. Everything was carefully prepared in order to make sure that each one of the visitors ended up converting into a believer: they hammered their brains with a constant discourse on the insolence of the state and the city, the same state and city that abandoned their national citizens and took in refugees without prior judgement; they offered clean clothing donated by third-parties to the homeless as soon as they arrived, but also as a gift to those who mainly came for food or hygiene products. The objective was to clean them up, to make them feel at home, secure, comfortable. The Captain's mantra was that to enter the Castillo one had to be first of all Spanish and second of all a clean and noble person. The definition of 'clean and noble' referred to the project's limitations, in no way did they want to resemble a detox centre for drug addicts, but also, and above all, they wanted to offer a specific vision of those who were worth saving from misfortune. Being physically healthy did not always go hand in hand with being in a good mental state, and they weren't naïve enough to believe that the mental health of those who came from living on the streets was excellent, no, the Castillo recognised this, and offered an opportunity for recuperation, gave people the opportunity to take back the reins of life. But they believed that nobility was found in precisely this positive spirit: the capability to overcome, take a step back and accept that the world as it was, was not the world you wanted. If someone had this capability to seek help, in the organisation's terms that could already be interpreted as a relative show of strength, a noble spirit, and a desire to improve. Not everyone would survive. In fact, only the best would get ahead, and it was the best that belonged to the list of those that were selected. Those who were too pessimistic, those with no desire to change, did not have a place in the Castillo.

In their work, it was often difficult to distinguish between those that they accepted as a charitable act – out of mercy – and those that clearly had some type of interest in the organisation, those who were useful for weaving, spreading, and propagating a network of influence and discourse. He remembered the Captain's words on the connections between the mouth and food: constructing dependent beings so that later, independently, they could spread the word. Santiago almost saw Sundays as a day of purification: a day to cleanse the souls and bodies of all of those present. The immigrants who attempted to approach them were politely diverted to the Red Cross or Cáritas as integrating them would have been a misdeed to the others, those who brought true horror stories with them: they were white, and only because they were white, because they were not foreign, they had no right to aid. Nobody knew how many of these stories were true and how many were lies, but that had never been important.

Santiago handed the list and the documents to the Captain so she could organise the line for the pantry. Her small voice was still the only thing that resonated with importance in the barracks. The collections were getting better and better every time, and now they were not limited to only food: they included sanitary products and sometimes nappies, baby formula. A young woman had started coming just a few weeks ago, she always came alone with her baby hanging off her hip, and some had made it clear that they would prefer it if they didn't help her as she didn't fit within the standards of nobility imposed by the Castillo. But the Captain ordered silence to even the slightest comments, and she ended up establishing a greater relationship of complicity with the girl than with many of the members. There were some in the Castillo who felt disgusted at seeing such a young girl alone, abandoned, and assumed that she dragged a gruesome story around with her, that she must have been some sort of sex worker, or at the very least an irresponsible girl. There were also some who saw the Captain's tenderness towards her as just another excuse to defame her. Santiago supposed they were right, in their own way, at least in the fundamentals: if the Captain was kind towards the girl, it was because she recognised herself in her, because she also brought up her son as a single mother, because she thought that it could have been her in that girl's shoes in any other situation. Santiago thought that the Captain was cut from a different cloth to the others, better, and he exchanged a smile with her when it was the girl's turn. The Captain took the baby in her arms, rocked him, smiled at him, played with him, blew raspberries, made silly noises; she tried to get a laugh out of him, a sign, something, a show of love. Santiago despised the others for thinking themselves so divine as to judge her. When they had closed up the food bank, he walked over to her and lit up a cigarette.

'Have you seen this, Santi?'

The Captain showed him an image: it was a statement written on a red background, along with the image of a young girl who wore a kerchief on which he could make out the hammer and sickle symbol. It used the hashtag #liberatedlavapiés and announced the 'expropriation' of the former Odeón studios in the centre of Madrid.

WHAT THE WORKING-CLASS BUILDS BELONGS TO THE WORKING-CLASS

After one week of occupation and works within the building the 'owner' appeared along with various teams from the national police in an attempt to enter the premises. We want to thank everyone who turned out to support the occupation of the liberated building in the Madrid neighbourhood of Lavapiés. Support and solidarity are the foundations of all collective work and are where our creative force resides; a force that we use to build and consolidate liberated projects in a world where the ideologies of removal and speculation reign.

There are many reasons a group of women and men have decided to start a project with the objective of liberating a dead and abandoned space, transforming it into a place that is open to the interests of those of us who continue to feel the effects of the financial crisis. We are united by the deepest conviction that we cannot wait around for someone to come and distribute the crumbs of a system that is nourished by exploitation and misery. We know that the law is not unbiased before anyone, that it is designed to defend the interests of the same exploiters and speculators who first got rich from the construction of the building, who later continued to do so with its producers, and who still do so today by speculating on a property that has been abandoned to its fate for eight years. But we are not scared.

As long as there are evictions, as long as people go hungry, as long as unemployment exists, as long as the rich are getting richer and the poor are getting poorer, as long as machismo continues to kill, we are going to fight to move this project forward, we are going to invest all our strength in building a more just, free, and equal world. Our determination is like that of all the generations that fought before us for our rights, of those who did not submit to resignation, of those who stood up and took a step forward.

We are men and women with burning hearts and the desire to build a world without oppression. We are a clenched fist, we are the red flag of freedom, we are the working-class, we are women, we are migrants, we are the Revolution.

'Does it worry you?'

'As if this is going to worry me! Santi, don't be an idiot, I showed you so you'd laugh. Did you not read the whole thing? It's fucking hilarious. "We are the working-class, we are women, we are migrants, we are the Revolution", bunch of little brats. They are completely irrelevant. Do you know what I've heard they're organising there? A fucking soviet film forum. They're sneaking into buildings with a big plan to project Eisenstein. Do you get it? Hearing that makes me even prouder of my work: could you imagine if all we were building here was just to show a Reifenstahl? They're just a bunch of little nostalgic kids who are playing at being revolutionaries: "look! look at me! I'm Stalin! Hey, I'm Lenin, I'm going to take the Winter Palace!" And then all they do is exactly the same as a little group of first year Audio-visual Communication students. "We know that the law is not unbiased before anyone", they say. You'll see, that suck-up on the city council, the one that says we're creating political insecurity, he's not going to say shit about them. He's going to keep his mouth shut like a little bitch. Because they're the sons and daughters of progress and they need a little bit of excitement in their dull worlds of private schools and Sunday afternoon pamper sessions.'

'Anyone would say that you're worried.'

'It doesn't worry me, but it does piss me off. The city council gets all high and mighty with us, yet they can set up their lefty drug-dens filled with Africans smoking joints… the exact same guys that will turn up at the doors of a supermarket with a knife.'

'I don't think we have to do anything, just let it pass. The anti-fascists will still piss us off, whether they have a private cinema or not. If they're so irrelevant they'll end up crumbling under their own weight.'

'I thought you were a better strategist. You're a smart guy, Santi, but sometimes you don't notice something until it's right in front of you.'

Santiago didn't know what the Captain was referring to. He put out his cigarette and made as if to leave.

'Stop, stop. Wait a second. Listen. Before, those guys had the Quimera, the Dragona, the Patio Maravillas, la Enrededera, a couple of places near here. But they were all already more or less established: they didn't have to clean anything up. We continue to be the minority, and we still can't trust each other. Our tradition is different, we're still growing, we're still not established enough, we haven't taken in everyone that we can, the football hooligans for example… But them lot, let's get back to them lot: they've just entered a huge, succulent building where they can hold meetings, get together, and coordinate themselves. But you know that the big guys are still pulling the strings: these kids can't do anything about it, but they know it's coming so they're all over the place. This is the perfect opportunity to put one of ours inside.'

'You're not suggesting…'

'You think I would ask you to do such a thing? You know I think a lot of you, Santi, but you'd be the worst mole in history. I'll sort it out, I'll find the right person. With the right amount of care, with the perfect actor, we'll be able to find out everything about the anti-fascist coordination before they even make a move; we'd have access to their names, even if they were false; to their addresses. If we got one of our own on the inside, we'd know everything we needed to give the necessary warnings, to figure out if we needed to break two legs or four. We could keep going until they knew that Madrid was no longer theirs. I don't care if the city council has been occupied by their accomplices, let's remind them that Madrid has always been ours.'

The days following the first moments of the expropriation were calm, and amidst the cold, one could hear only the sound of brooms sweeping and dust inundating the rooms, constantly moving from one side of the building to the other like a pendulum. Nothing happened other than repairs, construction, *revolutionary praxis*, daily tasks. The police constantly turned up to identify and frisk those who were in the building's surrounding areas, focusing mostly on its exits, but they were nothing more than little scares and there weren't even any altercations.

The biggest shock occurred a little while later when two workers from an electricity company appeared at the doors of the building. When the padlock on the shutter didn't give way, they tried to open it with a lever, at which point, alarms were raised. Vero and José ran to the door to face the intruders. The two men uneasily insisted that there was a fault in the street's power line that they couldn't fix unless they carried out works inside the building, and they needed to access it urgently. Vero quickly left to find some neighbours to talk to so she could prove that the company was just lying to try to sneak in. The police arrived to 'help' the two workers enter the building, but if it came to light that there were numerous people inside and that there was no problem with the supply in the rest of the street, they couldn't go any further, at least not without a court order. José later told them that one of the workers had approached him and told him that he had no idea what he was getting himself into, that it was better to leave the building sooner rather than later, as otherwise they would face the consequences, and there were certain families you didn't want to receive a warning from. José didn't give him the time of day. A huge banner, on which the words 'LIBERATED BUILDING' stood out in red was still hung from the roof to the delight of the neighbourhood and the working-class; at its side hung an enormous flag, a definitive sign of a demarcation of territory, of establishment, of absolute dominance. After the little scare was over, they continued cleaning because the restoration work was what truly mattered.

Accusations and criticism streamed in on social media. Trolls said that the occupation was nothing more than a group of radical sectarians, too attached to archaic symbols, to icons and idols from another time, to gestures of failed projects from a century ago. Ramiro knew that those words could only be uttered by someone who didn't have a clue about what they were talking about: neither the symbols nor their colours had ever mattered, but rather belief, faith, hope, the spirit that moved them, the emotions that pulsed through their veins and, of course, their history. A revolutionary's task, he would say, never started from zero: the history of the labour movement, of the working class was not just one of a few tiny contemporary fighters that surged forwards to war on the shoulders of giants, no, it was an eternal casteller that transcended time, a fortified tower of bodies that sustained themselves off the same cry.

But there were things that really hurt him. One day he received a friend request on Facebook from an older woman, about fifty or sixty years old; her profile opened with a sepia photo of a younger her, long hair, the colours in the photo indistinguishable from one and other. The message was a collection of reproaches. She described the organisation as a bunch of enlightened paratroopers who didn't consider the neighbourhood at the time of the occupation; she revealed, between spelling mistakes and long, badly written sentences, that the Odeón studios had been transferred to the association of mothers against drugs in Madrid so it could be used as a refuge and social centre. She insisted on the specific needs of the families from the Water Triangle in Vallecas – a shanty-town residential area of the city that was full of housing in ruins, buildings without electricity or air con, destroyed and damp. He felt guilty about what the woman qualified as a 'misappropriation' of the space, a shameless act, and she demanded that the building was returned to the association.

At first, Ramiro didn't let anyone know that he had received the message. He accepted the friend request and asked for the woman to give him some more information. She started to write him one message a day, soon two, and then they came in torrents: she sent endless messages about the history of the neighbourhood, about the mothers' thirty-year history, about the support they received from various parishes, and the appreciation they had felt, and still felt towards what they called the red priests. One day Ramiro asked her if she could stop sending messages and suggested they met face-to-face. She, María was her name, said that every Tuesday the association met in the Entrevías church, and that they could get together after one of those meetings. He gladly accepted and promised to buy her a coffee and she replied that she was already too old for that nonsense, although he seemed like a good lad, handsome, strong, and that she only had decaf, milky coffee. In a café close to the Assembly of Madrid, he met a woman with a tremulous voice and a multitude of grey hairs who was itching to tell him her story. She started to talk and got side tracked, picked up a thread, pursued it, dropped it and jumped from vine to vine, she weaved and undid the conversation, spoke about the help that the parish offered to those without papers or those in prison, those with dead sons; she told him of friends' husbands who had given in to drink, arriving home every day and every night stinking of red wine as a result of not having any other liveable life alternative within their reach. She told him about the three social centres they had been assigned, and about the constant need for more, about how help for addiction had disappeared, about the pain that this lack of resources caused, about the unending list of young people for whom help had inevitably arrived too late. María asked him to promise he would try to do something to help, speak to the others, put together some sort of agreement and Ramiro promised he would do everything in his power, knowing that it wasn't in his hands and that he probably wouldn't even dare to raise his voice, that he would obey and swallow what even for him supposed an injustice. He knew that he would never see her again, but that he would remember her stories forever, like he would always remember the wrinkles on her hand, the tight-fitting ring on her left index finger, and her dark indigo dress with white flowers, so similar to the one his grandmother sometimes wore. Yes, he would dare to do something. Upon his return to the building, he let the question slip.

Carmen replied. 'Oh yeah, we knew about it, and they would have done a really good job, they would have been really good people, but for someone to have given them the building, they would have had to have made a pact with the owners. And they must have got the money from somewhere. Do you not wonder why they have such a good relationship with the city council? Can you imagine the destruction of the neighbourhood they must have consented to because they think only about their own interests and not those of the rest of their class? In two weeks, the mayor will give them a new space for what they need, and they already have three, so I don't know why they want more. But in two weeks we'll still be here, building a community, fighting against labour exploitation, questioning everything. So yeah, we knew about it, and we would still expropriate the building a hundred times over. Happy?'

So much cruelty from her surprised him as one never imagined that that could come from such a fragile body: the capacity to pigeon-hole perspectives that were far from one's own world view with such a simple swipe, to consider nuances as irrelevant, to insist on holding a position without scrutinising the circumstances. He didn't bring it up again, but rather stopped there and let the guilt consume him as he continued, distractedly, to work on the posters for the activities that they had programmed throughout the coming weeks.

The objective, almost to make up for it, was to establish themselves as a place of reference within the neighbourhood, as much on a cultural level as on a political one, serving as a central nexus for the complex web of relations between the revolutionary left. The opening day had been a huge success, although it seemed too much like – for their taste, according to their objectives – a school open day. They soon realised that another one of their objectives had, of course, always been the possible recruitment of more activists. In the days leading up to the inauguration, the number of 'newbies' increased exponentially, and almost all of them were assigned to the central body. The organisation traced the cartography of *madrileño* territory and assigned place and position according to certain fixed borders: there was a centre in the north for the towns in the mountains, a central body that was nourished by Lavapiés and the areas with the highest population density, and a centre in the south based in Vallecas that recruited from the poorer neighbourhoods. The liberated building was established as the heart of this great organisation while the renowned Central Committee, ever in the shadows, acted as the brain. Ramiro would later come to find out that it had been the southern centre, with whom he had not had much contact before the 'expropriation', who had put up the biggest fight against the whole issue with the association of mothers against drugs thing, and that it was almost enough to cause a schism. It would not have been the first time that a group had decided to separate, nor would it be the last: if you dug around, someone would be able to tell you that the origin of the organisation went back to the scission of some activists from a sectoral grouping of the Spanish Communist Party, unhappy with the reformist, pact forming route the party was going down and, why not just say it, the social democracy that the party had adopted. Though Ramiro didn't know if this link was a source of pride or queasiness, of legacy or despair, he did understand that it prefigured a whole history of ruptures, separations, divorces of the all too often badly matched, and the imposition of other people's visions, tensions, and silences.

A multitude of organisations had responded to the Central Committee's call for projects, ideas, or proposals for activities. Not all of them were viable: the organising committee quickly oversaw the assessment of each proposal, not wasting too much bureaucracy or time, assigning various proposals a space (both in the buildings that had already been established, and the Odeón studios that were still in the process of being restored) and putting others to one side. An idea that went down well, following the model of so many occupied buildings, was the organisation of a charity coffee shop which they decided to place in the newly expropriated Odéon building. This involved the rehabilitation of the huge central room so the 'set' was cleaned and spruced up in record time and the blue canvas space of the old studios was filled with furniture donated by neighbours or found on the street such as benches, chairs they found in the store cupboard, and tables that had become old and had been chewed at or were missing a leg. They paid close attention to aesthetics in order to find a middle ground between the bourgeois-bohemian-hipster, and the scruffy decadence of many other *okupas*, relying heavily on ambiguity. They put up the regulation posters that declared that this space was absolutely free of chauvinistic aggressions, and comrades were responsible for decorating the space with phrases from Kollontai, Marx, Mao, and Lenin. *There can be no revolutionary theory without revolutionary movement, and vice versa. The red flag of the social revolution that, after Russia, flew in other countries across the world, proclaimed that the moment in which we would enjoy heaven on earth, the moment to which humanity had aspired for centuries, was close. It is clear what we must carry out in the present: the ruthless criticism of everything that exists, ruthlessness both in the sense of not fearing the results to which it leads, and in not fearing the conflict it will bring with those who hold power*. The 'anti-patriarchy' section added a few more later: *Capitalism has benefited from and continues to benefit from what we women cook, how we smile and how we fuck. The complete liberation of women cannot be achieved by separating itself from the fight against imperialism.* There were voices within the organisation that could not avoid being tempted by the refrain in their heads that denounced slogans and petit-bourgeois deviations from the united struggle of the working class and some complaints reached the Central Committee from members who considered that establishing an 'anti-patriarchy' section within the organisation reinforced the unacceptable dogma that the true enemy was within the party and not outside of it, within the system. The formal complaint stressed that behaviour and conduct like this placed all working-class men under a constant shadow of suspicion, from which escaping became an impossible task. Luckily and to much relief, some members (those whose great internal debate was whether to call themselves class feminists, or whether Marxism already prefigured feminism in such a way that calling oneself feminist would be superfluous) confirmed in the *petit comité* that those opinions against the anti-patriarchy section came from a minority. *Party discipline requires, among other things, that the minority submit to the majority. The minority, if its opinion has been rejected, must support the decision approved by the majority. If you deem it necessary, you can resubmit the matter to the next meeting for its consideration, but in no way should you act against the decision already adopted.*

It was in one of these charity coffee shops that Ramiro met a surprisingly cultured Fran, who chained together digression after digression from the constraints of his black tracksuit. Though he had never seen him at the neighbourhood activities before (because Fran lived in Bellas Vistas in the barrio of Tetúan), Ramiro was entirely captivated by him from the off and trusted him implicitly after just a few minutes of conversation. Fran slipped from one theoretical reference to another in a matter of seconds, demonstrating an exquisite knowledge of the material found in Marxist texts. Just when Ramiro thought he was speaking about the tendency for reformism and revisionism within the working-class, he would then unexpectedly and suddenly find himself in a conversation about the value of Marxism as a science and the misunderstanding of its extended dialectical success in some Marxist circles. He listened with fascination as he quoted Engels, and his definition of communism as 'not as a *state of things* to be established, nor as an *ideal* to which reality must adjust, but as a real movement that abolishes the present state of things'. He listened to how he spoke of Hume and the is–ought problem, which he interwove with Wittgenstein. He seemed to understand Marxist doctrine better than anyone Ramiro had ever met, including José, who organised the open reading sessions and training for activists. It didn't take long for Ramiro to suggest to Fran that he become a member of the organisation, insisting that he would put in a good word for him and pass on recommendations to the Central Committee, but his heart sunk when he realised that, due to where he was from, Fran would be forced to participate in the northern base, and not in the affairs of the central body. As they exchanged numbers Ramiro realised that the force of attraction he felt towards Fran was not reciprocated. He found no mirroring of his affections, yet he still wanted to continue listening to his words, even if they didn't amount to anything else, and he wrote down all the books that Fran mentioned, all the readings on the notes app on his phone. He did so with the tender mix of admiration and desire that one only experienced to the fullest between the ages of fifteen and twenty, something that soon disappeared when hearts became wearier.

Soon, the day-to-day management of the space became excessively burdensome, and everyone had far too many responsibilities to allow the situation to be sustained in the long term. In the assembly, it was decided that work assignments implied cleaning and the maintenance of installations, as well as the organisation of something practically every day. Mondays, yoga; Tuesdays, tango, feminist self-defence, yoga; Thursdays, a second feminist self-defence session; Fridays, charity coffee shop; Saturdays, charity coffee shop. Ramiro remembered the idea he had had to resurrect a cinema within the space, and realised that it was almost the most serious and formal of all of the proposed recurring activities. He brought up the use that they could give to a projector for the building in a meeting, only to be met with reservations. But they eventually decided that so as not to waste resources, and due to geographical proximity, they would move the projector located in one of the other centres to the expropriated space. Ramiro cleaned one of the old cinema rooms: he swept for whole days, climbed ladders to clear cobwebs, disinfected the room, ventilated it, and installed lamps, chairs, and tables. He proposed his plan for a socialist film series that would take place every Sunday at seven in the evening. The first films announced were Mikhail Kalatózov's *The Cranes are Flying*, Tomás Gutiérrez Alea's *Death of a Bureaucrat*, and Sergei Eisenstein's *October*.

The lights went out and silence was required; for lack of a better alternative, the projection stretched from one side of the room to the other, and a small cubic speaker with wireless connection transmitted the sound. Up came the image of the masses climbing some stairs. They tied the hands of the statue of the tyrant, mounted another staircase, and raised their rifles and sickles to decapitate the tyrant over and over again in eternal repetition – much like the repetitive cycle of actions that accounted for inevitability, for something that could never happen in any other way. *To all! All for one! Avant la lettre!*, explosive jubilation. The first three minutes of the film synthesised entire concepts and worldviews, intuitively explaining to any viewer that class struggle was the true engine of history. Accompanied by José, Ramiro explained how Marx took the notion of *clinamen* from Epicurus. It was precisely so as to resist the overdetermination and impossibility of change in social life that Marx imported randomness from nature: spontaneous displacement, the deviation of raindrops or their atoms if they all fell together.

Amid applause, *October* ended with an image of all the clocks from across the world, announcing that the time had come to extend heaven on earth to all territories. But then the image and the text contradicted each other: the film said that 'the workers' and peasants' revolution was over' and that this was the end, but the story said that the end was unknown.

Ramiro was satisfied. Some comrades congratulated him on his efforts: what were they? Search *October* on YouTube, project it by connecting the computer to a HDMI cable? Now he could see that he thought there would have been something more, that the liberation of the space would have meant something other than this dissatisfaction, this emptiness, this tedium. He remembered the disillusion he felt when he entered, how much he still believed in his project, and the weeks that had passed by without anything really happening. It was already the second semester of his university year, and he killed time as best he could: he read a lot, attempted to understand, underlined and persisted.

He read as he waited. He was back in the same café he first met María. They didn't even talk about the association anymore, but about other things, and she seemed to have forgotten that at first her messages had had a clear objective, an intention, a purpose. Now she recounted her life within a family who had immigrated from Seville, she described in great detail the road they had travelled, she explained how a population was distributed according to its origin and spoke about the waves of internal migration that all ended in Madrid. She repeated herself and insisted on telling him stories she had already told, but Ramiro liked to stay there listening, watching, quietly drinking his coffee and doing nothing. She always had to leave after a while and Ramiro would stay in the bar, sitting in a corner drinking his last coffee, looking at the mobile phone screen between his hands.

Height, weight, ethnic background, physical complexion, gender, pronouns, position, romantic situation. He was looking for a guy of whose existence he was sure among the ocean of grey squares, anonymous people without a photograph, sixty-year-old men requesting sex for money, photos of dicks, money for a picture of a foot with the big toe sticking out, praise for his youth. He continued scrolling through the intermittent positive reinforcement program and waited for a treat, waited, waited, typed, tapped and waited for the dopamine release. He had lost all sensitivity and no longer felt excitement. He tapped, tapped, waited, tapped, waited. He no longer responded to images.

He sent a few messages to profiles that could potentially belong to human beings with a soul or a heart, whilst he ignored the torrent of dogs in heat that pounced on his. He responded to someone who was two kilometres away – he had notifications for people who were less than five hundred metres away disactivated in order to avoid any awkward situations, encounters on the zebra crossing, little looks on the street. Ramiro responded to his 'hola' with another 'hola'. A mediocre response, he thought, but it was not like the other guy had played his best cards. He waited ten seconds. With the next message the guy asked him if he lived nearby or if he was just passing through. He checked his profile: there wasn't a face, only a well sculpted torso photographed from a favourable angle. He was white, approaching his thirties, but still settled in his twenties, taller than Ramiro, and asking for 'discretion'. Ramiro supposed that the 'discretion' thing – something to which he was accustomed – did not matter much to him; it was good to keep the 'discretion'. He stirred his coffee, tapping the inside of the cup with his spoon. Ramiro thought about it for a while and replied that he was passing through, that he didn't live in the area but that he could go up to his house and extend his passing for a while. He paid for his coffee and five minutes later was just about to get the metro when he received a screenshot of a location on Google Maps. The message that followed assured him that there were already condoms at the house. Ramiro told the guy it would take him about thirty minutes to get from Entrevías to Puente de Vallecas. He walked past the San Diego church, crossed Parque Amós Acero, the boulevard, Avenida de la Albufera. He didn't make eye contact with anyone he passed, he didn't nod his head towards beggars, he didn't feign a mutual understanding, he didn't grimace with disapproval. He arrived at Calle Pico Cejo, buzzed up to the flat on the intercom, crossed the interior patio, went up the stairs to the second floor – the lift was out of order – and knocked twice on the door. Santiago, who he was yet to meet, was waiting on the other side.

PART THREE:
LUST

Santiago would have liked to have been able to say that that afternoon he knew perfectly well what he was doing, that opening the door to Ramiro was simply one more step in the blueprint of a plan he had drafted, that there were to be no deviations because he had calculated every movement down to the finest details, that everything had been contemplated beforehand. He would have liked to have been able to say that his intention was not just a simple fuck or the release of some excessive energy, but rather – he dared to think – that his plan all along was to beat the boy up, break his body, leave him completely and utterly disfigured, rip him to shreds until he was no longer recognisable. Santiago knew, however, that no one would buy this ruse, so he fabricated an alternative tale. Man possessed certain biological impulses and from time to time – almost as a consequence of some sort of defect – those reproductive impulses could not realistically find a correct, concrete object with which to release themselves. Of course, these impulses were rectifiable, but rectification took too much time and work, and time was too precious to waste on rectifications, corrections, attempts to fix something a person could live with, something that didn't affect a person's personal or political life. There were several possible alternatives at hand that could eliminate those impulses. Santiago had at one point considered that one of those alternatives could be compulsive masturbation, but he didn't believe that a body could reach climax without being close to another, nor did he believe that extasy was possible without having absorbed or devoured other organs beforehand. What worked for him was sex simply for the pleasure of sex, orgasmic liberation as en end in itself, a way of releasing the tension; he saw it as a routine exercise, the reduction of the body to pure mechanics, rite and word incarnated in the flesh, discourse incarnated in substance and passion, an exercise through which the muscles, the bones, the flesh and the blood spoke, reasoned with one and other. Santiago never got with anyone who lived too close, and he always asked the guy in question if he lived in the neighbourhood or was simply passing through. He would always set his home as the meeting point, because even in the shadows of the night other people's spaces were suspicious. After the act he would block every single man with whom he had shared fluids; he would delete him, cross him out so as not to repeat him; he didn't share any information with him, he wiped him from his memory. He never allowed the exchange of more than a few of the most necessary words, he didn't tolerate tenderness and he didn't accept it when the other insisted on showing that there was a soul, a voice behind their body, that there was fondness, a motive, that there was anything more than simple impulse or desire. He needed the other to remain just a series of palpable tissues or textures that could only be traversed with the hands, the fingers, nothing more; he needed to forget everything that lay beneath and beyond the curves of their body and leave aside the disturbing thought that this was something more than a simple imbalance of chemicals, something more than just a piece his mind was lacking, something more than banal energetic impulses that were triggered and would irremediably lead to the end. Santiago opened the door to allow Ramiro inside; he took in the figure stood at his door, noting the almost soft normality, the eyes, the legs that were slimmer than his own, bonier and bowed, almost muscle-less. He took in the gazelle-like features of a body that had been hunted by a multitude of predators, the bags under the eyes, a sure sign of not having properly slept out of fear of these predators, resorting to just taking short, five-minute siestas that were plagued with paranoid thoughts. Every door that did not lead to his bedroom had been closed; he had carefully cleaned for the occasion, wiped his internet history just in case, aired out the place, and disinfected each and every corner so that everything was clean before he dirtied it again and it would have to be purified once more. They entered the bedroom and Santiago stood still, disarmed and frozen, just looking. He stared at Ramiro, only his eyes moving, and he almost panicked when he thought that even his involuntary movements, the automatic ones, would be interrupted. He apologised when he realised that Ramiro might have noticed that he had frozen, and explained that it usually didn't happen. Then he commented that he had read on Ramiro's profile that he was a bottom, as if requesting confirmation. He received this confirmation, although Ramiro admitted that he was more of a vers than a bottom. Santiago replied that it didn't matter and threw Ramiro down onto the bed so they were both lay on their backs. He undid Ramiro's belt and touched him in small, circular movements; he heard him ask if there wasn't going to be at least little bit of foreplay, at least some sort of tenderness beforehand. Santiago replied that that would happen when he decided it had to. He watched Ramiro's sweet erection rise, contemplated the vein that ran down it. It was larger than he had expected, but slim, and tight at the base, very different to his own, and he could not avoid his own. In a sudden, swift movement, he entered Ramiro, and still inside he oriented himself so he could search for the lubricant with his hand. Upon finding it, he then found Ramiro, and began to touch him as he moved his body with rhythmic, calculated movements, enjoying the sensation. When he could hear that the pleasure was becoming excessive, when he realised that Ramiro was enjoying himself too much, he moved his hand and lifted it to his neck whilst he was still inside him; at first he squeezed it gently to hear him moan, then he gripped it with more force, almost as if he were attempting to lift Ramiro's body by the neck, as if he were attempting to shift the whole world from just the flesh he had a hold on. All the movements Santiago made now originated from the force of this grip; Ramiro's neck was carefully squeezed, clenched right up to its breaking point, just far enough. He shifted his free hand back to Ramiro's penis and continued squeezing his throat so he could feel the bulge of his Adam's apple, until Ramiro finished all over the towel that had previously been placed on the bed. He slid his penis out without releasing his grip on Ramiro's neck and lifted his own torso up so he was positioned upright on his knees; he waited for Ramiro to follow him so he could fill his mouth. He felt Ramiro's lips move closer, they were just millimetres away, his tongue playing happily with his head. It was as if they had rehearsed this routine for months, it didn't appear that this was the result of pure spontaneity. They continued in this position until Ramiro took the initiative and pulled away, taking Santiago in his hand until he finished all over his face; he licked up the drops of semen that dripped from Santiago, that were being released never-endingly. Ramiro carefully cleaned up, Santiago was convinced that he wouldn't stop until there was nothing left to squeeze out. Santiago jumped up from the bed and ran to the bathroom leaving Ramiro alone. He got in the shower, closed the screen, turned on the water and allowed it to fall on his body without even waiting for it to heat up, without waiting for the boiler to kick in. He closed his eyes as the water poured down on him. Using the wall to support himself, he breathed, tried to empty his head, tried to think of nothing at all, tried to quickly put a stop to any images that flashed across his mind. He persevered at this – failing – for ten minutes. After wrapping himself in a white towel he walked into the hallway and was immediately filled with panic when he saw that the door to the living room had been opened. He discovered

Ramiro sat on the sofa half-naked and wearing the same boxers as before – they were now dirty, there was an area of an unidentifiable radius in which Santiago could make out a pre-cum stain, and the bulge was still surprising – with a cup of coffee in his hands, and the pot on a tray on the table. Santiago turned white. He asked Ramiro what the fuck he thought he was doing, already aware that the response would be stupid, idiotic, aware that he would be reduced to describing the perfectly observable act of preparing coffee. Later, Santiago would come to understand that this very act implied going into the kitchen, and that upon entering the kitchen Ramiro would have seen the occasional photo of him and his father, the dirt, the grime, the gas oven with its greasy, rusty stains, the beige extractor fan that dripped as if it were excreting bile, the fridge filled with fruit that was always on the verge of moulding, of being consumed, the drawer full of poor people's clutter, the *magdalena* cakes that he snacked on three by three, and that upon seeing all of this, Ramiro had still prepared the coffee, found the tray, and laid out everything for Santiago's reception, like the perfect little maid he had always lacked. He received the obvious confirmation that Ramiro was simply making a coffee, with the cherry on top being that he added, or at least insinuated that he didn't appreciate Santiago's coldness and indifference that much, that he didn't appreciate sharing his bodily fluids with someone and then having them turn around to say, *alright, goodbye, have a good day, if I see you, I won't remember you, I don't know you*, especially given that he had thought they had a nice connection, that they were cool, that they had had a lot of fun. Santiago asked him to get out of his house. Ramiro did not move an inch. He was silent, not a word came out of his mouth. Santiago insisted that he left at once, nobody had given him permission to open the doors that had been closed and invade his intimacy, his personal space. They had only fucked, nothing more. At this, Ramiro left, trembling like a little puppy, scared as Santiago slammed the door behind him, got out the Sanytol and started disinfecting, disinfecting, disinfecting.

The general historical trajectory of life in Madrid was a steady, unceasing march towards the total eradication of tenderness: another form of disinfecting surfaces. The trees, with the passing of the years, had been replaced by emptiness and absence, the grass and the earth in which they had grown in a previous life had turned into concrete, tarmac, open pit ovens. The earth had been scratched away and peeled back so it could be better enjoyed by cars, by all forms of private transport; gardens saw themselves replaced by pavements and roads, pavements and more roads as Madrid exterminated everything that once made it an old Manchego *pueblo*, hopelessly succumbing to the siren song of modernity to which it pledged allegiance. Madrid, in a nutshell, was a parody of this very modernity, a joke made in bad taste, a playful transformation for the gentry, nothing more than an exercise in attraction and aggressiveness and mockery and ridicule. In the modern world, all ideas of heritage were reduced to ashes, so the city needed to constantly start from zero and forget itself, it always needed be ready to bury itself. In doing so, it continued – with the utmost tenacity – to endure as the city of the dead, as a necropolis without sanctity, a villa and court of corpses of falsified boulevards and sprawling parks worthy of the Sun King. Madrid was an entire city dedicated to extermination and assassination. Its public spaces were chipped away at day by day until it was forgotten that once upon a time they had ever existed, robbing anyone of the memory that these spaces were, and could have been different. It is only logical that, having fewer spaces in which to exist, and finding fewer spaces in which to love, people loved themselves less, or at least they loved in different ways. It was irremediable to think, therefore, that in trying so hard to destroy itself, Madrid had also destroyed its inhabitants, and in destroying itself, it had ended up destroying love, turning the city into a great machine of cruelty, an insatiable sphere of consumption, an apparatus of special coercion, an instrument that was only useful as a form of government. Madrid was a terrible angel, death disguised as something else. Car, after car, after car, after car, weightless bullets pierced the metropolis, racing from one side to the other and leaving only ruin in their path. Madrid was a glimpse into the cities of the future, cities that would not be developed with human beings in mind. It established itself as a role model: this is how you make a whole population forget that the fortifications that belonged to the past were once kind and not just oppressive.

Santiago knew that he was a contradictory victim, that he had participated in the construction of his own circumstances. He could criticise the wasting away of human relationships all he liked, but within all of this decay, he had found the only way in which he was able to relate to other people in a viable way without excessively laborious, sterile, useless explanations. He understood that, after not so long, the same mechanisms of coldness that he used to sleep with other beings would become generalised, and even those who did not realise that their impulses or mechanisms were bound to perversion would disinfect each of the surfaces touched during the staging of their acts. He believed that soon the connections between disparate individuals would become nothing more than a thumb that distractedly played with small grey grids on a phone, searched for photographs, investigated positions, pigeonholed. He used his usual method for another three afternoons. For another three afternoons and evenings he placed a towel on the bed in the same way, attacked the bodies of others in the same way and threw himself at them from similar angles, but for all his efforts he only got different results, and in none of the cases did he find the absence of love and attention as exciting as it had been during that time with Ramiro. He thought the feeling would end up fading away, but it didn't, and he found himself remembering certain parts of Ramiro's body with fondness: he thought of his ears whilst he was doing something else, and his heart skipped a beat when he read a similar name on the list of the homeless taken in by the Castillo. And then he felt the disappointment, indifference, disdain at seeing another face. Eventually, he also missed Ramiro's insolence and audacity, he imagined his hands frantically searching for the correct shelf, opening the coffee pot, dismissing the world, preparing everything without knowing the correct proportion of coffee to milk, to sugar, to anything. He despised himself and turned to others so he could make himself hoarse from screaming at the top of his lungs. Any misstep could have quickly turned into a defeat.

How could Santiago explain these feelings, these thoughts? He found himself searching the internet for different justifications. Every now and then he looked at the /polgbt/ thread on 4chan, a kind of /pol/ guerrilla raid on the /lgbt/ subforum, which it claimed as the /pol/ enclave for 'gay guys who were right-wing, conservative, anti-SJW, *red-pillers* or from /pol/'. The discussion topics varied:

>*that feeling when you don't have a right-wing boyfriend*
>*coming out of the 'right-wing' closet in the gay community*
>*Milo or Trump: who has the best hair?*
>*other famous gays from the right*
>*self-defence tips against muslim homophobes*
>*that feeling when you don't have a fascist boyfriend*

>*that feeling when you don't have a boyfriend you can talk about your internalised homophobia with*
>*that feeling when you don't have a boyfriend you can take to the woods to practice shooting your pistols and rifles and shotguns*
>*that feeling when you don't have a right-wing boyfriend who likes feminine boys*

When he had finished scrolling all the way down to the end of the screen, he came across a completely different point of view.

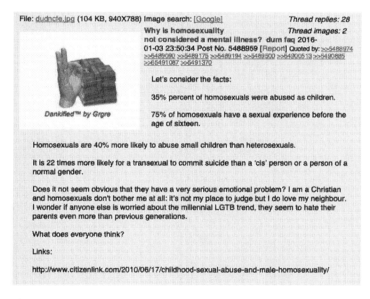

File: dudncle.jpg (104 KB, 940X788) Image search: [Google]   *Thread replies: 28*

Why is homosexuality   *Thread images: 2*
not considered a mental illness? dum faq 2016-
01-03 23:50:34 Post No. 5488959 [Report] Quoted by: >>5488974
>>5489090 >>5489176 >>5489194 >>5489500 >>54900513 >>5490885
>>65491087 >>5491370

Let's consider the facts:

35% percent of homosexuals were abused as children.

75% of homosexuals have a sexual experience before the age of sixteen.

Homosexuals are 40% more likely to abuse small children than heterosexuals.

It is 22 times more likely for a transexual to commit suicide than a 'cis' person or a person of a normal gender.

Does it not seem obvious that they have a very serious emotional problem? I am a Christian and homosexuals don't bother me at all: it's not my place to judge but I do love my neighbour. I wonder if anyone else is worried about the millennial LGTB trend, they seem to hate their parents even more than previous generations.

What does everyone think?

Links:

http://www.citizenlink.com/2010/06/17/childhood-sexual-abuse-and-male-homosexuality/

Dankified™ by Grgre

The hypothesis was supported by statements from a certain Gregory Cochran, a physicist and associate professor at the University of Utah: homosexuality could find its cause in a pathogen, either a virus or bacteria. The justification for this referred to its low inheritability rate (fixed at 0.22), its absence in hunter-gatherer populations, its high frequency in the Western world (approximately 4%), and the unfeasibility of a possible evolutionary explanation. That a male had no interest in females, nor did he aspire to reproduce, constituted an evolutionary handicap. If his impulses were caused by a 'gay gene' it would already have disappeared, as it did not result in any type of reproductive effectiveness. The frequency, compared to other case studies such as with redheads or cystic fibrosis, made it impossible for it to be a mutation. In addition to all this, there were several examples of infectious agents that altered behaviour (as was assumed of homosexuality): rabies was an amplifier of aggression, influenza promoted sociability in humans before the first symptomatic manifestations, and toxoplasmosis caused rats to experience a sexual attraction towards cat urine. The hypothesis that homosexuality was the result of an infectious agent not only served to explain the existence of homosexual people, but also accounted for homophobia as a straightforward aversion to them, with this having a higher inheritability rate than homosexuality itself (0.5). Homophobia also had a very specific intent: it occurred in greater proportions where homosexuals had contact with children, and in these cases homophobia prevented the pathogen that caused homosexuality from spreading among young children. In the same way, according to studies, the degree of discomfort people experienced in regard to homosexuals increased if they were homosexuals who worked with children, such as paediatricians or child-psychiatrists. The contagion mechanism of the pathogen was not entirely evident, since it was not very clear if it was transmitted by sexual relations; the only thing that could be known for certain was that a period of prolonged exposure to an infected individual would ultimately result in the transmission of the infectious agent. Homophobia would thus fulfil a clear purpose, linked to the unconscious and civilizing defence of reproduction. Homophobia prevented children from being exposed to the infectious agent that caused the inversion during the window of time in which their sexual orientation was modifiable, that's to say, it had not settled and presented vulnerabilities or weak spots. There was no other possible explanation, given that the existence of homosexuals should, in non-infectious conditions, end up serving as a help or benefit for the rest of the men in the community, by reducing the competition for the females. The conclusion was promising: the possibility of finding a vaccination for homosexuality. Another person added, on the same thread, that yes, there was a possible explanation from the perspective of evolution: population control. A third commented that the most probable explanation had nothing to do with a virus or bacteria, but with factors like diet, stress, physical health, or an excess of oestrogen in bodies, the atmosphere, and other similar elements. They stated that the excess feminine hormones in society could perturb men's natural sexuality. A fourth, looking for a conciliatory path, attempted to unite in one explanation the effects of an external pathogenic agent and prenatal exposure to certain hormones, citing the effects of the order that brothers are born in: the more older brothers a boy had, the greater the probability that he would be homosexual. A fifth explained that homosexuality was nothing more than a psychogenic phenomenon based on the absence of a typical gender identification, a consequence of the power that women had acquired in the face of men, thus 'deconstructing' the natural dualism of the masculine and the feminine. This being the case, man was unable to identify himself with masculinity, with power, and so acquired – as a result of not feeling worthy of the apparently superior females – a serious inferiority complex, devaluing women and idealising males, thus trying to achieve masculinity through the submission of the rest of the men in the world.

On other threads, there was talk of '*sex for pleasure* between men who were not homosexual', considered by some to be 'the most normal thing in the world'. In order to be able to fall within this category it was necessary to follow the fundamental principles of the doctrine, its commandments. The first was to consider this type of sex as a pastime, a bit of fun without much meaning, something that did not, under any circumstances, lead to the development of feelings, care, or tenderness. One also had to ensure that during the sexual exchange there were no kisses, affectionate gestures or eye contact, in order to avoid any possible interpretation by oneself or the other that something other than the simple sexual management of physiological needs was being carried out. It was also necessary to commit these acts only when it became absolutely essential, without settling into any form of routine. It was important to ensure an absolute annihilation of all tenderness, to perform only simple sodomy without the exchange of words or glances, and reject typical homosexual behaviour. It was necessary to consider sexual activity as a simple outlet, and to have a conception of the other as simply a receptacle of orgasms with which to unburden oneself. This explanation was not very convincing, for him or for the rest of the forum members. According to Bulldozerbass, 'not happy with the goats, the moors have brought us new customs'; according to ATARAIXO, 'sex is just a load of rubbish that consists of rubbing bodies together, it's nothing more than a massage. Sex as an act is nothing and only holds importance because it creates addiction, it's like a drug, it transforms the mind, producing attachment in order to bind together a couple and allow them to last long enough to raise children. A stud pig on a farm experiences sexual desire as soon as he hears the worker who is coming to extract his semen with a mechanical straw, it doesn't matter if that worker is male or female. Most of the world are sex addicts. Marriage is a form of celibacy and, given that the pleasure and joy of living is produced by the multiplicity of sensations related to the fact of being alive, sexual desire is nothing but an urge to reproduce.'

Santiago knew that something within him was not quite right, and he would not allow a couple of behavioural excuses to prevent him from observing in great detail the complex mechanisms of his perversion. The story with which he most identified, though he carried out some of the practices described in the thread about 'sex between men who are not homosexual', was that there was something inside him that was irreparably broken, a mechanism that, once activated, could not be stopped. He was fully aware that his desires and biological purposes did not coincide with the natural principles that he worshipped, yet he preferred to fold to them rather than try to bend to the norm; he preferred to free himself in the shadows so as not to spread the false assimilation of a variant that sooner or later he would have to extinguish. He felt disgust at seeing two men holding hands in public and felt a burning sensation in his stomach when he thought about how the frequency of these apparitions had increased over the years, even in his neighbourhood. He found it difficult to come to terms with the violence of the noise of the cars and the noise of the streets along with the noise of those people performing little flashes of gratuitous, obscene tenderness. He carefully stored this violence, classified it, turned it into a routine, accepted it as a fundamental component of his life and existence, claimed it for himself, extrapolated it from the rest of the universe, transformed it into a general rule or measuring stick, and injected into his veins what was left of its existence. Santiago was something of a fanatic or a prophet who was devoted to his cause, and his position had varied over time, making almost pendular movements. For months he thought that homosexuals were not necessarily part of the collective enemy that needed to be exterminated, accepting the emergence of trends such as this as a more or less inevitable phenomenon within social life. Yet even when he thought this, he would always condemn his own acts, repeating to himself that there was something more important above, insisting on the need to zealously pursue the reflection of his image in the world, sacrificing everything else if necessary. Then, following long debates with himself and reading and rereading other theories, he came to accept the *feminising* and *oestrogenising* trend of the contemporary world as, among many others, a device that was used to control society, a cultural invitation to a collective fainting or forgetting, a symptom of decadence, the shadow of substitution from one population to another. He consoled himself: at least he had never liked blacks or moors, beyond porn, beyond some videos, (access to which he had soon restricted so as not to fall into temptation, installing extensions capable of preventing access to certain categories on certain pages). The object of his desire was not a simple conse-quence of biological seedlings, liminal impulses, but proof that, although not completely transformable, some components of human life that sprouted crookedly from nature could become straighter, corrected, controlled, submitted to the tyranny of the individual mind. He thought that hell too would pass and that, if it didn't, it wouldn't be necessary for him to do anything, because he could just forget about it. Nothing could be done at that time.

Ramiro walked under the flower arch and sat down on one of the benches beneath the pergola. A Latin American maid quickly came over to ask them what they would like. He had not interacted with many maids in his life: it surprised him to think that some people could live day after day with someone who played, among others, the same function as a waiter, although this role was extended to servant. He had friends who were waiters – without realising, did he also have friends who were maids? He asked for a tea and listened as she reeled off a long list of all the possible options. He decided to opt for the easiest and most specific: rooibos with milk. For milk there was also a list: rice, almond, coconut, quinoa, walnut, hazelnut – the recommended variant – canary seed, spelt, cow in its respective variants, percentages, and lactose contents. He didn't feel like experimenting and asked for a splash of normal milk, semi-skimmed, observing the little painting formed by the milk that had already been poured with such care into Lidia's cup.

How had he got here? They were already in the second semester. He had met a charming, porcelain girl in class, who wore long floral dresses and collected her hair in a plait that fell to one side, with whom he discussed politics and leftist dilemmas; they ended up making an effort to correspond their schedules, share notes and help each other out. Ramiro was glad to have a little bit of company at the university. One day, he had asked her if she wanted to go with him to a party in Lavapiés. Lidia said she lived quite far from the centre, so it would be too difficult for her; Ramiro wasn't convinced. One day, as they drank a small beer followed by a coffee in between classes, Lidia told him that she had something to confess, something she appeared reluctant to share, as if it would have to be ripped from her mouth. She spent a while slowly wandering her way through a barely strung together preamble: she tried to disseminate all the leftist content she possibly could on social media, she did what she could, she had no other option, but she could not demand her family to use their money for what she would use it for, nor ask them to renounce their properties... It was money, it turned out she was rolling in it, what would have run through her veins in other times was not blood, but gold, and in the present moment, her blood flowed with stocks: her family was one of the richest in Madrid. He wondered if the contradiction ate away at her, he questioned how she could want all of those like her to disappear from the face of the earth. He didn't ask her these things, not because he didn't want to, but because it felt incongruent. Instead, he asked her if she could really desire the disappearance or even the death of her own father. Of course, the answer was no. He then asked if as a result she could still be considered a revolutionary. The answer was the same, but she added: perhaps even in revolution killing cannot be justified. Ramiro thought that her answer wasn't that bad, and ignored the voice in his head that told him he was letting himself get swept up by bourgeois, moralistic tendencies, by a pacifist degeneration that only served to justify daily capitalist atrocities and legitimise social differences in reinstating the commandment: do not kill. He smiled again, now with a little more understanding; he wouldn't tell his comrades that his new friend was a posh little rich kid.

The reality was that Ramiro, like a large proportion of those involved in these type of projects, did not come from poverty or the precarious sentimentality of the traditional proletariat, nor did he share its dirty tics, its badly formed habits, its slightly incorrect way of sitting, of always keeping leftovers, of calculating the weekly shop down to the last penny, of grinning and bearing it, of repeating dinners, of not having good manners, or ignoring polite house rules. His comfortable middle-class life had allowed him to develop an interest in political, almost religious projects with the fervour of someone who was immediately able to extract a way of acting and a way of life from them. Within these projects he found a morality that he could export onto the whole world and use to instruct his life and train the feral. The problem was not how his origins might alter the structure of his thoughts or the schemas through which they were formed, because the mental configuration of the poor and the 'normal' did not present so many differences; the fundamental problem was that Ramiro lacked anger, hatred or pain, and whatever anger, hatred or pain was within him was simply a posture, never a real wound.

Ramiro, therefore, supported Lidia and her contradictions and was able to afford to do so. He was not wrong to, in fact, as it was sustainable to affirm that the moral position of those who did not feel like killing was superior to that of those who would be willing to take up a rifle. The middle-class itch was by no means universal in the Commune; in this realm of the poor, there was an abundance of dispossessed people who sought to gouge each other's eyes out rather than have a debate about their viewpoints. He had always been aware that there was very little that bound him, for example, to Carmen, and deep down inside each of them, there was something that prevented them from singing the same slogans or chants. They were separated by a crack that they would never name or speak of out loud: a little wrinkle in class, a crease that allowed them to reach different standards of well-being and comfort, a crease in possibilities and dreams and respect, crease upon crease. Carmen worked as a waitress – there it was, he had found who the maid reminded him of – in dodgy bars in Lavapiés that still hadn't fallen victim to gentrification, bars that resisted modernisation, bars in which there was no music and the shouts of the landlords slid over the grease of the crisps to the toilets, then back, without washing – time stood still in these places. Only after so much work did Carmen have time to be an activist, organise things, move from activity to activity. She slept the absolute minimum, only what was strictly necessary to withstand the roughness of the next day.

Lidia dissected the Madrid elite as Ramiro continued to gaze in amazement at the garden, the fountain, the artificial lake, the grass, the dog, the pergola, the flowers, the vases, the contemporary sculpture – nothing tacky, it was tasteful, a kind of round and curved W, a concave made from white marble. His middle-class itch reappeared, revealing itself for what it really was: it wasn't perfectionism, but the desire to take absolute advantage of the social ladder, the social ladder that always went up: unlike drugs, this desire did not produce relapses, and it never emerged as a conscious manifestation, always remaining just below the surface, like an amphibian that refused to leave the water. Lidia told him about the Florida Retiro bar, about the families she met, about famous people she could tell jokes about, about little lines of coke, rose gold bracelets, champagne, Abu Dhabi, an island dedicated to techno, a lot of bad taste and worse consciences. He told her about some of his experiences in the Commune, he spoke about Eisenstein, smirking when he said that he would have asked her to attend one of the screenings, but now he better understood her reluctance to go down to the Madrid of the masses. He was well aware that these rich districts of the cities did not venture into their parallel worlds, that although the borders between them were delicate, these flows between districts were but an illusion. Every public space existed under the threat of invasion, and now he had infiltrated the upper-class Salamanca neighbourhood. He didn't know what was more difficult: staying there, or protecting the Commune under fear of the police.

Lidia, still in the depths of her demarcation effort, talked about some of the associations to which she secondhandedly contributed donations after convincing her family, she told him of a building that they had set up for an NGO in El Viso, about friends of her parents who hoped to wash their consciences clean by setting up organisations so they were able to sleep at night believing that they were doing something for the rest of the human beings on the planet. She revealed, after a while, that she knew the nephew of one of the owners of the old Odeón studios, and that she had found out they were slowly beginning to prepare legal action with the objective of vacating the building after the summer. Alarm bells began to ring for Ramiro as he felt as if he had been cornered like a rabbit in the headlights: he had spoken to her about his participation in the liberated space and knew that she could give his personal details to the family that owned the building. She downplayed it, said that there would be no evidence, that she totally supported his work, that she didn't believe that it constituted a crime, and that the nephew in question had already pissed her off just a few days ago: she defended social work tooth and nail and praised squatting as a public service vocation. Ramiro cracked up at the idea of squatting being a 'public service vocation' because he had never thought of expressing it in those terms, not for even a second. He asked Lidia if she too was not washing her conscience clean, criticising her rich peers so much, dramatizing her excessive support for the benches of the radical left. In the same way that he would not tell his comrades that his new best friend was loaded, he would tell hardly anyone about his escapades to that oasis, escapades that were becoming more and more frequent.

Ramiro told Lidia about the guy he had got with, the guy for whom he had absolutely no contact details, just his Grindr profile. He told her that more than once, he'd thought about turning up at his house, but he'd never gone through with it. It would be a bit creepy, she said. Ramiro told her that the guy never responded anyway, he didn't even read his messages. Lidia advised him to wait, suggesting there was little more he could do, and asked him if he felt like going out that night. Ramiro was shocked: she had never shown any interest in going out with him before. She replied that she had been playing with the idea for a while and that, at worst, she would dress up as a proletarian, like in that film about the princess and the pauper. Ramiro didn't find that funny.

For some reason, he sought to entertain her, a feeling that always emerged in those subtle stratagems of seduction that unfolded at the beginning of friendships. His first thought was to take her to the centre of her world, to a centre that he assumed she already knew, to choose a place that was both elegant and bohemian – their ideals were practically antagonistic, but not excessively so. He thought about finding a place that didn't resemble a trap for the nouveau riche or the liberal professionals of Ponzano, a place that blurred the lines of comfort with low-voltage lamps and an industrial appearance. They ended up in a place on the corner next to the Plaza del Duque de Alba, a place that was somewhere between a bar and a cider house, with chairs that were visibly prettier than those of the trashy joint a few meters away where the taxi drivers grabbed a bite to eat. Ramiro drank a beer, and Lidia chose a glass of white wine, asking carefully about the bottle and demonstrating her inherited knowledge at all times – the kind of knowledge that was not acquired at university unless there was somebody present who was willing to exercise symbolic domination. They stayed there for a while, comfortable, laughing, in intermediate territory, until Ramiro received a message from Vero asking him where he was. He embarked on a long line of negotiation to convince Lidia to go down to Lavapiés. She didn't scream crazily that she was afraid of being raped, but she might as well have, and Ramiro preferred not to further examine the implications that she might be afraid of being raped in that specific neighbourhood, but he could imagine. They continued in a methodical tug of war until Lidia conceded, and they saw out the plan.

The walk from La Latina to Argumosa was not long, if perhaps a little hostile for heels. Once seated at a table on the terrace, Ramiro introduced Lidia – who looked like a secret spy between the lumpen and the hipsters – as a classmate from university. Vero was wearing a sloppy sweater and a bum bag. She asked questions and pointed out Lidia's idiolect, her haughty, bourgeois way of speaking, the fine-tuned lilt of the aristocracy, but she closed her mouth before she pissed her off too much. Lidia played along and offered her well-honed responses, she compared anthropological disciplines with what Vero studied in Social Work and joked that all social sciences were a variation of each other depending on how far away you wanted to be from your study subjects, that's to say, from misery. Lidia's laughter was stiff and false, but the alcohol loosened her rigidity and allowed for a miraculous truce between classes to be signed for a few hours. The truce was on the verge of breaking when Lidia brought up the subject of Santiago, Ramiro's big secret, of which he had told Vero nothing: for a few moments it seemed enough motivation for her to threaten to get her things and leave. The threat still remained but the drama was resolved with a long explanation. Ramiro recalled the story of their meeting and Santiago's current absence which was, after all, all Vero had wanted to hear. Sides were then taken and Lidia and Vero each assumed their roles. Vero seemed to think this guy was a dick, without even knowing the ins and outs of his relationship with Ramiro or his actions, which she for sure would have interpreted as perverted. Lidia was initially more understanding, allowing Ramiro's infatuation to contaminate her own point of view and hoping, like him, that the flame of love lasted more than an instant. The girls shared stories of confrontations with dodgy guys, or the dissatisfaction of one-night stands, and they reached the pragmatic conclusion that in the end it didn't matter what story Ramiro told himself: if Santiago wrote again they supposed that it might even be worth it, that he might prove to be something more than just another twat. And if Santiago didn't respond, it didn't matter, as the thought of another good fuck would soon be enough to erase the biochemical ecstasy that was generated by an orgasm.

The bar was closing soon, and finding another place on a Tuesday night would have been almost impossible. Lidia was drunk enough to accept being taken to La Huelga, but the place was empty and they went out to smoke just a few minutes after going inside. Without considering its drawbacks too much, Vero suggested going to the *okupa* on Plaza Nelson Mandela, just in case there was a dj or a party there that night. Lidia laughed and whispered something in Ramiro's ear about her limits, although he did wonder for a few minutes if she'd give in. They went back inside La Huelga: Lidia walked uncomfortably up to the bar on her tiptoes and, much to the disgust of Vero, asked for an Aperol spritz. Ramiro, more accepting, ordered them two beers. They drank without paying much attention to the music, talked about banalities, love, and the proletarian revolution. They decided to go home as soon as they'd finished their drinks. Vero announced that she had class tomorrow and ran off to catch the night bus in Acacias. When Lidia finally saw her disappear into the streets that went down to the South, she ordered an Uber to take her back to her territory. She offered to take Ramiro back, too, but he explained that he lived so nearby he could just walk. With his friends already far away, happy with the magic he had spun in coordinating a new meeting, he walked the few streets that separated him from his flat. To distract himself in the middle of the night, without looking where his feet fell, he used the last little bars of his battery to open Grindr. A message from Santiago popped up.

He ran home and put his phone on charge.

Santiago had not blocked Ramiro. To install padlocks and clamps on those shoots of desire would not have been enough, he would have had to uproot them completely from his life and prohibit all reappearances, which was something he did not do. He would repent after his self-denial, his lack of abstention, chastity, or capital virtues, but of course we already knew about his affliction and were well aware, thanks to the confessions of sinners, how much these afflictions affected people like him, his way of dragging himself through the world wouldn't be enough. Dejected and pitiful, following one night of misery after another and without getting his hopes up he had reopened the boy's profile, their conversation, and found several apology messages sent by Ramiro until he gave up. Then a miracle: he was online. Santiago couldn't resist the impulse and typed, waited, waited, typed, waited. *I was an idiot and I'm sorry. I spoke to you like shit. I don't usually have that sort of intimacy with strangers or people I don't know from Adam. To be honest, I don't usually have that sort of intimacy with anybody, I'm not used to it. I'd like to see you again. You can come over to mine. I live in the same apartment you've already explored, the one with the closed doors and shut off spaces you intruded. You already know where the coffee is, so we're off to a good start. What's your name? I'm Santiago. Please, whatever you do don't call me Santi, I hate it. What do you do? I study anthropology,* Ramiro replied. *Ah, like a good friend of mine. Oh, what's her name, maybe we know each other?* Santiago had to deflect, the Captain was identifiable. *No, she's already graduated. Ah fair enough, so what do you do? I'm preparing for some government exams. Which ones? At first I thought about going into teaching, as there aren't many options with a Philosophy degree, but the idea of having to go into a school sounded unbearable to me. I studied law too though, so I'm preparing to enter the Superior Legal Body of Lawyers in the*

Administration of Justice. It sounds shitty. It is, but I've got a lot of time to kill. Why law and why justice? Santiago had to deflect again. *An attempt to put right what is wrong in the world. And what do you think is wrong in the world?* Deflection. This guy was a lefty for sure. *Economic inequality, social injustice, poverty, the misery suffered by so many whilst no one does anything about it.* Would Ramiro find that attractive? Was Santiago really dealing with a liberal? He didn't think that liberals could possess such tenderness, nor that they could transmit with just a glance of the eyes those little beams of light and compassion. The eyes could say so much, and so shamelessly, even when it was impossible to focus on them for more than a few moments. He was called Ramiro. He was an activist in a communist organisation. *I'm not an activist, I don't have any faith, or any of that particular energy,* Santiago replied. *Is activism a matter of faith for you? Yes, but not just that. You're from Vallekas right? Wouldn't a little commitment to a cause be normal for you?* Ramiro asked. *I don't know where you come from, but sometimes outsiders have a distorted image of reality, and around here there's no ambition, just ramshackle building works, billboards, loose tarmac, scaffolding, helplessness, neglect, shortages: there are those who dream of ambition, but the rest of us have enough to keep ourselves alive.* Have you ever walked through one of the little working-class towns in Spain, Ramiro, Santiago thought? Have you not noticed the total absence of those pedantry temples for books? Have you not noticed their replacement... no replacement no, because they never existed in the first place, but have you not noticed that in those places only tiny shitty stationery stores exist? In the churches there, the images function as substitutes: they replace the codes within the sacred books so that they are legible, so they can be extended to the majority, to those who cannot decipher ink, so those people can recognise in the frescoes the same tales that are offered up by their priest. People in those places don't read, they hardly even dream either, so those dreams have to be instilled in other ways: there are entire towns in which no one is expected to end up taking an interest in books. For places like that books hardly exist. There are only hints of the written word and a loop of infinite sadism allows the deluded to set up book-swaps in disused telephone boxes or little cupboards thrown together on the side of the road; all this to improve, to improve themselves, to attempt to make their children love something that because of their caste or social stratum they never could. They were activists, if you could call that activism, not in order to correct their lack of culture, but to correct their absence of life, a life which is ours. *Why are you an activist?* Ramiro would have liked to think that he was a activist for the same reasons Santiago was preparing for the legal exam, but lately he didn't know. *I want all my actions to have the best possible results, I've always wanted that*, Ramiro said. *I don't think people normally speak about this kind of stuff on Grindr*, Santiago replied. *Yeah, you're right. But it's almost five in the morning, and I'm not gonna get out of bed at this time to come to your house. Why not?* asked Santiago. *Because we all have things we need to be doing tomorrow. Yeah, that's true, so, what have you learned in Anthropology?* Santiago thought about what he knew about anthropology. Levi-Strauss said that in India, the Muslims had only constructed temples and tombs, uninhabited places, human less, lifeless; he said that this reflected Islam's inability to think about solitude. On an aesthetic level, Muslims were puritan and reduced sexuality to its smallest forms, like scents, lace, gardens. On a moral level, they feigned tolerance as they exhibited proselytism of a compulsive nature; contact with those who were not Muslim distressed them, and they lived under constant threat from the rest of possible existences, freer than theirs, looser. This quote is thought about, remembered, but never spoken aloud. Interesting, Santiago thought. Islam seemed to be a method used to develop insurmountable conflicts within the souls of believers, only to save them later by proposing excessively simple solutions. Just a thought. Ramiro finally responded. *I learned the other day that we falsely accuse primitive societies of believing that the rites they performed would have effects. In fact, sometimes they performed rituals simply to mark a suitable moment, the passage of time, like someone adding a note on a score knowing that the symbol will be left there, abandoned, and whether the note is performed or not the music, will continue to play. These societies knew that their rain dance would not make it rain, but they recognised that there would still be storms, so they danced without believing that their acts were those that caused anything. The symbolic effect was pure beauty, precision, exercise of the body, but without necessarily wanting to alter the order of everything. Order is altered with patience, waiting, listening.* Yeah, that's interesting, Santiago lied. *Don't you think we do a lot of things like that, knowing that something won't have any effect, that it will change nothing in the world, not even our perception of it, but we still do it all the same, as if something were going to come out of it, pretending, almost playing or acting?* Ramiro added. *Yeah, perhaps.* The metaphor was a little stretched, Santiago thought, the comparison was hardly transcendental with the daily life of activism and its processes. Santiago decided that he would take affection over boredom any day. Or maybe in a situation such as this, he preferred the idea of producing admiration even more: together, they could exercise their memory muscles, boast to each other that their knowledge was more profound, impress each other with learned codes, readings that, in their day, were depreciating, show a chameleonic ability to appear as something, hide and suddenly reveal oneself as another. *Do you want to meet up tomorrow? It would be nice to have the person I'm speaking to in front of me. What time works for you, and where? At your place again? Yeah, that way we can try to improve on the last time. Finish better. That would be difficult. Ha ha. Shall I bring coffee? I have too much here. Bring beer. Deal, see you tomorrow. Do you think people normally speak so much on here? No, I've already said that, especially not about these kinds of things. Shall we watch a film? Let's see what we end up doing, for now I just want you to come... you know, this was difficult for me, it took a lot of effort to write these messages to you, because at the beginning I was absolutely incapable. How odd, you're a few years older than me, right? A few not many. Don't go thinking I'm a predator or something like that. There's only four, five, six years in it, nothing more. Yeah, I mentioned it because it's strange, you've got a few years on me, but it was still hard for you to reply to my messages, write to me, accept that I'd made a coffee while you showered. That eternal shower thing was also bit weird. I would explain myself to you, but you wouldn't understand. I'm bad at it. Let's just leave it at that: as something I'm bad at. Ok, will you give me your phone number? I don't know why you want it. So that the next time we talk, if we talk again, I can call you. I think I can count the words you said to me when we saw each other on one had. It left me wanting more.*

The next day arrived and at first there was no sex, just a triumphant arrival with some cans of beer. Ramiro entered the house – whose address he found by going back through their conversation on Grindr, although he almost remembered it by heart – insolently, as if it had become his property. He placed the cans on the ground, looked for the fridge, opened it, made room and put the cans in, one after the other, looking for the cold. Santiago hated smiling, but a smile slipped out, a smirk, *because this was more than just beer, you know, something like this it sticks to you, living where you live and showing up with beers, just like that, as if it were nothing, on a Thursday after-noon.* The mere appearance of this smirk could have justified a bombing or murder: how dare Ramiro provoke such reactions, do those things, bumble around like a charming goofball? Santiago's contempt was logical: a natural reaction to knowing that he was no longer acting on instinct, that his objective was no longer just the simple release of a certain charge or accumulated sexual tension, that the game had complicated itself and reached levels that should never even have been considered. In no way did he address Ramiro in such a way that revealed himself, no, the accumulated disgust came to affect his interior, curling up on itself, like a kind of reproach that had been formulated and intruded his mind over and over, an alarm that did not stop sounding, a persistent tinnitus. Ramiro was more of a child than a Bolshevik: his dominant emotion was not some kind of communist fury, but a fresh tenderness, still raw, sculpted with great difficulty by life. He drank happily, smiled abundantly, and drew all the light that filtered through the blinds of the apartment towards him. He was just as delicate and attractive with clothes on as without them, he lacked tics, if anything, he had a very slight regular spasm, nothing more than a tremor that produced itself in his hands after he had chain smoked two cigarettes.

They spoke a lot, and each realised that they were great orators, it was as if they sought, whether they wanted to or not, to cajole anyone who was listening to them. Santiago continued to hide many things, skilled in the art of constructing lies, but he started, every now and then, to let slip some truths. They were not forced or the result of false affection, but rather small escapes of thought that found their ideal receptor in Ramiro. One had to bring up the coldness that the other professed for his father, his condemnation of rubbish, his obsessive cleanliness, his mother's absence – which was not made explicit, though could be easily assumed – and his need to always be distant. The other complicitly took in lively re-enactments of petty bourgeois dramas and the fantasies that stirred up households in which both parents practiced liberal professions, accepted the other's networks of contacts, his inheritance, the world he had at his fingertips, and his use of radicalism for aesthetics. They would talk until things began to get intimate, and at first Santiago always shunned this, but with a bit of insistence, his body and other proximities ended up being the most interested, and later it was often he who initiated eagerly. From time to time he stayed at Ramiro's house, who shared a flat with a girl and a boy his age, on those occasions sleeping on the sofa. He had made it clear from the beginning that the idea of sleeping next to another person was unbearable to him. Ramiro woke up with Santiago in his bed just two months after they met. The time they spent together allowed them the possibility of caresses, tenderness, and the desire to share more spheres of their lives with each other, extend the domains of their relationship, a term that neither wanted to use for different reasons. Ramiro considered it almost archaic, old, unsuited to his historical moment. On the contrary, as a mark of self-respect, Santiago did not even want to admit the possibility of having something as serious and institutional as a *relationship*. Santiago systematically rejected each one of the invitations Ramiro extended to him to attend screenings of the socialist films, go to the charity coffee shop or events with his friends, even simply to get a beer on the terrace of any city centre bar. He justified all of this by pointing out that he preferred that neither his father nor anyone close to him knew anything about them, that he feared – he couldn't give more of a shit, that was never the important thing – how they would react. He claimed to be prioritising a well-being that would benefit both of them, but only if they settled for silence and lived clandestinely within the confines of their bedrooms. Contact with Ramiro's roommates was more than enough, and before them Santiago was immaculate, well-rehearsed. This muddle ended up becoming a huge source of frustration for Ramiro who confronted Santiago on several occasions, insisting on how under no circumstances did he want to become a kind of 'mistress' or 'little secret' that Santiago could enjoy in private, on his own terms, and explained how it was impossible to think that Santiago could actually love him when he systematically refused to show him or show it in general, how difficult it was to think that Santiago could love him when he had not even once said *I love you*.

A narrative thread woven in this way conveyed the impression that everything was more or less going well, without any major mishaps. Of course, there were some typical difficulties, but difficulties that were sweet given that the shipwreck was shared. But, ever tenacious, reality reared its head to remind us that some pitfalls kept the relationship on the constant edge of the abyss. The condensation of so much time, summarised in the previous paragraphs, does not allow for the transmission of the clear images of those days, cloaking – as if it were a game of shadows – each of the protagonists, disguising the contours. Santiago often disappeared for a day or two. It had nothing to do with his obligations in the Castillo: it was just the kind of eclipse that was demanded by living a double life. Ramiro learned not to ask where he was, not to go to his house, not to inquire, not to need him. Sometimes this rift felt different: upon Santiago's return they would walk side by side in silence without saying a word, Santiago's face completely blank, his steps cold. His answers, for hours, were binary, and the most significant gesture that Ramiro could get out of him didn't even amount to indifference. From this emerged numerous therapy sessions at Lidia's house, who was dying to meet the lucky man and felt almost responsible, by way of magic, for his reappearance in Ramiro's life. She changed her mind every couple of days: her advice on Tuesdays was that Santiago was probably a dickhead, her advice on Thursdays turned into a psychoanalytic speculation about what someone with pretty screwed-up flaws could be like as far as intersubjectivity in relationships went.

In any case, in each one of those moments – those storm clouds or instances of fog – Santiago knew that whatever this thing with Ramiro was, it had no possible future, it couldn't last, nor could it have a happy ending. Not because they were different – though that they were – not even because he had never contemplated that the relationship could last over time – because denying it in such an unequivocal way would be a lie – but because he knew that beneath the structure of whatever they had was a swamp of un-confessable secrets, little ideas that he could never share, a swamp that was preventing the person with whom Ramiro was falling in love – because he was falling in love, there was no doubt about that – from bearing Santiago's name, or anything like it. He accepted his sentence and resigned himself to it: his plan was to relish the relationship as much as he could for as long as possible, to allow himself to enjoy it and bask in the calmness, to wait, wait, wait.

When was the first *I love you*? Four months into the relationship. Santiago seemed happier, he was sleeping more, his eyes were brighter, he was eating better, he even cooked, having forced Ramiro to delete every single delivery app from his phone. They often read together and shared books, even if Santiago censored some of his own readings that he kept hidden in corners of his house or in a locked folder on his computer. On the rare occasions that Ramiro happened to see an open document that appeared suspicious, Santiago would make something up on the spot: a story that he was just reading out of mere curiosity, following up on a philosophical-political interest that sought to confront everything. Ramiro was convinced that Santiago was just as on the left as he was and had never questioned his affirmation, only his core ideas. They did not avoid political and social debate, which were occasions for which Santiago had developed the perfect character: he embodied Ramiro's radicalism to camouflage his own, mixing the odd element of national chauvinism with Stalin in order to disguise the real meaning that he gave to the term *nation*, shielding some controversial opinions with the mishaps and necessities of *realpolitik*, showing a frontal opposition to the typical good-naturedness of the hippies, the progressives, or the social democrats, and by denigrating supposed postmodern or neoliberal tendencies that appeared within the proletariat and typifying them as the symptom of a struggle between the aristocratic working class, comfortable in its position of power, and the authentic working class who were resisting their absolute engulfment by capitalism. Fired up, they approached and withdrew from each other during their discussions, facing each other, at times almost shouting, Santiago always measuring his words so as not to go too far. From time to time he insinuated, based on what he had heard from Ramiro and his new and varied positions in the debates, that Lidia's influence on Ramiro was almost more perceptible than his own, mocking that he would soon have to come out of the closet like a dirty social democrat. Time and time again they would resolve their differences by leaving words aside and going straight to sex, which caused Ramiro to very solemnly declare that love was counterrevolutionary, something that immediately caused Santiago to laugh, which in turn unleashed his own shame, leading the two to end up in bed holding each other.

Ramiro said it, in short, when he thought that Santiago was

already asleep, when he thought that he couldn't hear him. He whispered *I love you*, into the calm of the bedroom and waited for an answer that did not arrive. He instantly knew – the silence that he did receive would have been ever so slightly different if he wasn't – that Santiago was listening.

Call me Santi, please, I'll let you. I told you I hated it, but that wasn't true, I only let one other person do it, my best friend, and she almost forces me to, but I'm asking you: can you call me Santi? Well, I don't know if I feel like it. I like to contradict you, it's too much fun, so fuck off. Then they kissed, Santiago feeling that this world could suddenly make up for some uncertainties. One undressed the other in quick movements, they rushed tenderly at each other, and their bodies became a playground where flesh and sweat frolicked. They pursued each other's necks and blood, they conspired – in the day, yes, during the day too – against the change of colours that mornings imposed.

Santiago was surprised to find himself doing things that he had never imagined he would. One day he prepared coffee as Ramiro showered (this time no one left) before they went out together to get something to eat – although he insisted that they did so in certain areas and still rejected public displays of affection. One night, Ramiro achieved the impossible: they went out together. They began the slow march from the abysses of the south, climbing the rotten roads of Atocha, pressing against the wall surrounding the Retiro park, clinging to each other to combat the cold that from time to time concluded the cruel nights of Madrid. They were late because of Moyano, because they walked up and down that little hill with the kiosks – now shuttered up, the books that spilled out during the day crammed inside – and sat on one of its cement blocks that served as a bench. They played, beneath coat and coat, at capturing a kiss between jackets, at untying the knots of their scarfs and caressing each other just a little more, almost clawing at each other with their hands while they laughed, revelling in the future that still showed itself to them in clear, credible images, capable of fulfilling them. They arrived at the club stuffed with the cold and well wrapped, they left their things in the cloakroom, they held each other's gazes carefully. Between the bass and the noise, Ramiro introduced Santiago, his friend, his boyfriend, *he's my partner*, he introduced him, he showed him off. Santiago, refusing to dance, stayed at the bar and ordered a bottle of beer, paid for by Ramiro.

And where does your money come from? I've always liked that question. Most people get really nervous when you ask it. Where does your money come from, Ramiro? Let me guess. It's strange that we've never spoken about it, isn't it? It takes a surprising amount of time to talk about the origins of money. Let me guess. Are they civil servants, your parents? Teachers? No, my dad works in the Tax Agency and my mum's a teacher in a secondary school. So predictable! And yours? Santiago took a swig from his beer. *My money doesn't come from anywhere, you already know that, I pretty much don't have any: my dad's a binman, he deals with everyone else's rubbish, he herds bins and bags, porous and dripping, as if shit were his cattle. My mum's not around. Where is she? It's not time for therapy, all that matters is she's not around.* Hence so much anger, Ramiro. Do you understand it, the rage? You don't. Because you lack anger, hate and pain, and whatever anger, hate or pain is within you could never be a wound. It's not a bad thing: I envy you, but you will never be able to understand that part of me. You will carry on praising utopias, you will continue wanting to make the world fairer by moral imperative, but what will heat up in you will never be your blood, what determines how much effort you make will never be your blood, your veins will not swell, you will not want to die in the attempt. You're even frustrating: since you appeared I hate less, there are no small atrabilious haemorrhages festering within me anymore. This part of the conversation played out only in Santiago's head. *I'm going to dance for a bit, Santiago. Cool. Come with me? You already know that I'm not going to. Go on, dance, I'll watch you for a bit. Have fun. I'll be here.*

Between the shaken ice and avoided glances, Santiago thought about how it was not only space that imprinted itself on bodies, but temperature too, with all the subtleties and implications that its symptoms carried. The cold always brought its own meanings, its associations with ice. The heat was different, its spaces as hot as the core of a planet, alternating between solid and liquid. The night, with temperatures lower than the day, was divided into requisites of depravity with the objective of fleeing from itself for simply a moment in time. All the bodies that danced exuded a heat that could not stand the surfaces of their bodies and this heat spread like aura and fire, it propagated and its magnetism attracted the heat of others. Ramiro's naked torso among the others did not inspire desire, but jealousy: the unbearable image of the body of the possessed moving to the rhythm of indistin-guishable shadows, between lights and shadows, silhouettes, and nights. But Ramiro was ecstatic, one among many, he dissolved into everyone following the electric cadence like robots. Santiago did not see himself as capable of stopping that great machine of desire. He left the empty bottle on the bar and went out to smoke.

They found each other after a while at the exit. *Hey, Santi. Hey. Your pupils are dilated, Ramiro. Yeah, I'm boiling too, it's normal. You didn't tell me you were going to take anything. Well, I didn't think I had to tell you. I normally do when I go out like this, I thought you would too. It's not the same without anything, I don't enjoy it as much sober, I don't feel it the same. But it's just occasionally. Isn't it a bit sad that at your age you already need substances to enjoy your night? I hear your preaching, I hear your morals, but I'm not ready for that at this time of night. I'm telling you because I love you: I don't want you to be a sheep, dependent. Really, Santi, really? I knew you weren't enjoying yourself, but you don't have to ruin everyone else's night too. Nooo, because you've been propping up the bar all night, staying away from everyone else. Lighten up a bit, loosen up a bit, have fun, don't be a bore. Forget it, Ramiro, just forget it.*

Santiago went back to Ramiro's place alone that night, opening the lock with the copy of the key that he had given him, and inhaling the scent of the sheets that he wrapped himself up in so as not to miss Ramiro too much. He consoled himself with the scent, a substitution in the presence of segregation. He still hadn't fallen asleep when he heard the door open. Ramiro slid into the bed, hugging Santiago tightly. *I missed you so much between the heat and the bodies,* he said, *that I decided to come back for you early. What are we going to do if it becomes a habit, this missing you too much? I don't know. But we'll learn to control it.*

Santiago trembled for fear of losing this, and Ramiro tightly held what was left of the embrace.

The Captain told him his head was in the clouds. The frequency of errors he made on the lists for the food bank was increasing exponentially, dossiers had begun to get misplaced, and he had also began to miss some of the food collections. Alejandro, the neo-Nazi who had been chosen as the mole – corpulent, built like a brick shithouse, constrained by a straitjacket in the form of a black tracksuit – joked around with him, asking if he'd finally found a girlfriend, and insisted that he introduce her to the rest of them, that she couldn't be that hot. Santiago didn't make it apparent that comments like that irritated him and he undid the rumours, shooting them down and repeating that he was just focusing on the day-to-day. The others laughed. There was a meeting called at seven in the evening, the objective being, in the Captain's words, to inform and warn everyone about the Castillo's next steps.

Illuminated by the now-merciful April sun as it broke momentarily through the rain, the inner circle entered the food bank. Among those present was a curious balance of factions, a reflection of the underground struggles for power and control of the organisation: the only representation for the hooligans in this type of over-intellectual encounter was Juanma, who acted as a link with the rest, participated in the decisions, and then transmitted the orders to each of the executing arms. Alejandro and his team covered the Nationalist Socialist quota, with more brains than the brutes – though with similar motivations – but little influence for being too radical in their ways. The theorists, like Jesús and Borja, were never lacking. Alejandro lit a cigarette and passed the lighter to Santiago. Everyone present showed the greatest respect, and no one dared to speak until the Captain had spoken.

'Jesús, come. Come, come, come here and read this aloud, if you'd be so kind. No fear, just go for it.'

Standing in the middle of the room, The Captain handed Jesús a garish pink sheet of paper emblazoned with an antifascist flag and something like paint marks on the back. Jesús read out loud as The Captain marked the pauses with punctual interruptions.

Our platform is made up of different groups and organisations that have united forces to combat fascism, racism, sexism, and all existing forms of discrimination. Groups from the extreme right have not disappeared, nor are they a thing of the past. In fact, they have increased on all levels in the last few years both on the streets, where they contaminate the popular classes with their message, and in institutions, where they reap the fruits of their trade in manipulation and lies.

'Do you hear this, comrades, do you hear this? Thanks for the recognition, "friends"! The "groups from the extreme right" they call us! But if that victory is ours alone, the conquest is ours alone! We "contaminate the popular classes with our message", they say: we'll see how much their "fight against all forms of existing discrimination" matters to the popular classes! And the institutions! But the institutions are governed by their accomplices!'

Their objective is to divide the working class through xenophobic discourse, blaming the economic crisis on migrants and refugees instead of the large companies who increase their multi-million profits year on year and who, together with liberal politics, have led us into the utmost precariousness, along with a completely disproportionate loss of rights and freedoms.

'I repeat: do you hear this? No, it's something else completely: rather, do you smell it, like the predator that smells the blood of its prey, its wound?'

To achieve this, they are using the same strategy they used almost a century ago, the same strategy the institutions use: violence and fear mongering. This is something that becomes palpable with the increase in the number of attacks of a racist, homophobic, and transphobic nature in the last months throughout the entirety of the Spanish state. Making use of the most despicable opportunism, they take advantage of the attacks carried out by their counterpart, Daesh, wrongly called the Islamic State and, with the same dishonesty, blame the entire Arab and Muslim community for their actions, despite the fact that the main victims of Daesh and the majority of their attacks come from Arabic countries from outside our xenophobic borders.

'Our "xenophobic borders", yell this posse of fanatics, these snowflakes! They believe that all our civilisation's problems will be solved if we allow thousands and thousands of moors to come in and stab teenagers and rape our own women, as they did in Cologne, as they will do everywhere. They want to turn Spain into a training camp for jihadists, just as they have done with Belgium. They say that we defend the big companies, and they don't even realise that they're the ones who obediently abide by each and every one of the guidelines set out by the most brutal globalism. They are crying and crying out for criminal gangs to bring over cheap labour with which to drive everyone to misery, left to fight over the scraps. They call our legitimate defence "despicable opportunism", they call our courage to tell the truth "violence and fear mongering". And what about them? What about when they turn up in gangs to intimidate us so that we can't collect food for the homeless? Is that not violence or hatred? Or maybe it's just called submission? Look, they are incapable of stating the name of their country. They can't do it, it's too much for them… and they think they are better for not doing so! They say they defend the people: the people from which imaginary world, from the Spanish state?'

Faced with such a situation, our platform rises as a response to this scourge attempting to divide a working class that has historically been, and still is, multicultural. Proof of this are the foodbanks found in the neighbourhoods, as well as the freeze on evictions that has been in place for years. Dozens of groups and organisations have already come together to show that our city is not a home for fascism, and that racism, homophobia and transphobia have no place on our streets.

'Forgive me, comrades, but I hear their cries and they seem so tender, so naïve. These posh little commies tell us that the working class "has always been, and is, multicultural"… and then proceed to describe exactly what we do! Who feeds the Spaniards when they prefer to abandon them, always serving their owners, so easily manipulated at the command of their leaders? Who is there when the police want to evict a Spaniard, a patriot, a good man, or a noble woman? Fascists, they call us! Racists, homophobes, transphobes! Our only concern, and you know this well, has always been to be patriotic and serve our people. They say that we have no place on our streets when every day we are more, and every day more people open their eyes, wake up and smell the coffee: they are the ones that have no place, because they are sick, abnormal, godless, cynical. We will beat them! Because they accuse us of the very thing that defines our pride! If defending Spaniards from the barbarism of nihilism, relativism and materialism is being fascist, then we will shout: "We are fascist!" with pride. If keeping the flame of tradition alive is being fascist, if not allowing their degenerate ideas to spread is being fascist, if the pain you feel when you see your motherland in danger is fascist, if making the values of truth, reality and tradition visible is fascist, if today's revolution is fascist, then we will shout: "We are fascist!" with pride! Long live fascism, burn the shapeless world that they defend, death to their barbarism and degeneration! Long live fascism!'

The Captain let herself get carried away by the shouts, the cries, the voices of others, thus exposing a flaw in her pride, a small sin of vanity, a chink in her armour. The mood became so heated that some began to raise their arms, bellow louder, drive themselves crazy. The same idea crossed Santiago's mind again: the entire script he had written could fail, the baton might slip from his hands. He had trained the Captain in the art of allusion, subtlety, trained her to understand that double-codes, in order to work, must also be cultivated within groups, meaning that excesses and impulses were corrected and unreasonableness was subdued, like using an ultrasonic whistle on a dog so that no one barked more than was strictly necessary. But there, in that moment, in order to get a louder applause, to produce a rage capable of creating enough energy for a few cities, the Captain seemed to have forgotten all he had taught her. In an attempt to reach silence and extinguish the fire, she told them that soon it would be time to scream for real. She asked Jesus to finish reading.

In the coming months, we will carry out various protests and hold cultural events, sports events and recreational activities in different parts of the city, to which we invite all those organisations and groups that want a city that is home for all, and where Nazis and racists have no place.

'Silence now because I need your attention: we've reached the most important part of the meeting. You are all aware, we've been planning it for a long, long time, that on the 21st of May, the third anniversary of Dominque Venner's suicide, patriots will rise together with one voice across all the largest European cities in order to defend their territory, their traditions, and their identity against terrorism and invasion. They already have more experience of things like this in other countries, but it will be our debut: everyone must stick absolutely rigidly to the plan so we're able to launch it with maximum violence. Do you know what these idiots do, what they offer us as an answer? Alejandro has been among them, and he has already had the cunning to discover it: next week they will call a counterdemonstration to confront ours, they will paste Malasaña in posters against Naziiiiiiiiiism, the fascists, how intolerable racism is in our neighbourhoods. These good for nothings want to declare war... and I know how tempted you are to shout back at them about what kind of war they will get! I get it! But don't let them drag you down: we're not protesting against them. Do you know what they've put down in writing? That the only way to stop fascism is by breaking its legs. We know they want us, those sons of bitches. What I want to make clear is that every single one of our acts, every single one of the organisation's acts, after the demonstration, of course, and never during, will have to be… in legitimate defence. I already see the smiles. You know the rest: during the demonstration, there can't be any raised arms or exalted shouts. The only thing that should be on your mind are the Spaniards that we house here, in the Castillo. No violence. We want them to see us for what we are, who we are: people who protect their people, who give them shelter, food, a little clothing to wear, a helping hand, Spaniards who are reborn among the helpless, the poor, those who have nothing. We want them to see us for the nation that we are. And then let's see if they are shameless enough to shout in the face of the evicted, wishing, like the fanatics that they are, that they get out of their neighbourhoods, longing for the humble to die because, in their eyes, if they are Spanish, they are scum. But what the hell: they're not going to react, they will remain completely withdrawn like the violent and hate-filled machines that they are.'

Just as with everything else, Santiago had been the ideologist behind this idea of minimal drama between protesters, of the immunity stratagem, a method with which they would become untouchable players. This stratagem, this manoeuvre, rested on a difficult balance – which he considered practically impossible but with which he had to deal – between the responsibility and self-control of all the other attendees, their intelligence, and their ability to step aside and not monopolise the limelight. But the Captain announced it like the idea was hers, her conspiracy: Though Santiago would choose cunning and camouflage a thousand times over if the alternative was violence without intelligence, she preferred to make the copulative conjunction of that phrase resonate, stating that one had to be violent *and* intellectual, that the State was useless without the greatness and power of the one who carried the axe, without the threat of violence, but Santiago believed that violence was useless, it didn't serve the State. He was worried about how close Alejandro and the Captain had got ever since she had chosen him as the mole to infiltrate the Commune. He knew that Alejandro's and his proposals, methods, and ideas about what to do and how to do it were antagonistic, and that either one would win or the other would, but both could not take control of the organisation at the same time. Pull the strings from the shadows, he whispered in the Captain's ears.

In theory, as in many other cases, the revolutionary organisation imposed a certain criterion of discipline and integrity. Traditional and sacrosanct values, family values, were, of course, exalted, but at the same time it was communicated that no member could get carried away by friendships or family – or any ties for that matter – and must be ready to break said ties without thinking about the cost that the rupture would have on their personal life. In practice, it was something else completely, and Santiago knew perfectly well that on the few occasions in which a female activist had managed to enter the circle of the Castillo, some of the hooligans had behaved like she was in a raffle or lottery and looked to see who she could belong to. The respect expected from authentic revolutionaries was in permanent revolt against the modern world. His indifference on those occasions also came to provoke jokes and mockery from the brainless sector and he knew that some of them called him a faggot behind his back, just because he didn't aspire to fuck every newbie that walked through the door. He was not surprised that the Captain and Alejandro had asked if he had gotten a girlfriend, because the *de jure* prohibition did not have any kind of *de facto* application, and all of them did what they wanted in their free time, whether or not it was a true example of patriotic praxis. But Santiago pushed aside these questions and focused on the organisational issues and tedious bureaucratic exercises: he prepared and studied the route of the demonstration, coordinated with other organisations that were less active than theirs, but were essential to exhibiting some kind of muscle in the capital. If Ramiro noticed he was absent, Santiago alluded to the nineteenth-century-esque, grotesque syllabus of his government exams, hiding his true concerns under mountains and towers of paper, pages, and notebooks.

Weeks before the day of the demonstration, they discovered that an army of moths had invaded the left cupboard in Santiago's pantry. Taking out one of the jars that were infested by about fifteen larvae, they extracted them with toothpicks before depositing them in a container full of vinegar in which they slowly drowned: the worms writhing first in violent spasms before slowly, unhurriedly, hunching over with convulsion after convulsion until they stopped moving and began to turn a deathly brown colour. While Santiago struggled to rip off the cable supports, free the wiring and look down the back of the cupboards to see if there were larvae – at least one, two, three pieces of corpses and cocoons must have fallen during the brutal blows of the operation – Ramiro took advantage of the moment to slip him a few questions about his friends, using the moment to doubtfully raise his suspicions, and affect what he could affect. The winds seemed kinder since the first time they had gone out together, the conversations had sweetened with drinks, and confidence had grown, while paradoxically the crumbs of secrets became more indigestible. From time to time Ramiro saw the tremble that remained on Santiago's face after he had hidden something, covering its possible exits, so he attempted to poke gently, as if pulling one thread would unravel a thousand more, insinuating that no relationship could work if truths were not disclosed.

Santiago did not give in and always found a new excuse. Ramiro wanted to demonstrate his lie, expose him, but none of his strategies gave him results and as they methodically extracted the larvae, all his comments fell on deaf ears. Santiago panicked when he found one crawling the edges of the table, far from the cupboard. He checked with the torch on his phone that the rest of the kitchen cupboards were spotless and took out the jars, tins, utensils, checking everything exhaustively. Santiago supposed that some of Ramiro's suspicions were unavoidable: when one invested a superhuman effort in cleaning and ordering, when one controlled oneself excessively, the remaining tasks that one is surrounded by begin to crumble apart with small errors. Sometimes Santiago suffered from forgetfulness and, carelessly, he wouldn't notice that something had already been done, so did it again as if it were the first time. He would also often forgot one of his years, his days, his months, or what government exam he was supposed to be studying. Did Ramiro really believe that exam story? Santiago supposed not. He couldn't believe, at least, that someone with apparent leftist commitment was not attending the demonstration. Did he have a fear of violence? Ramiro tried to calm him down. Santiago laughed. Had something strange happened to him, did he have a difficult story to tell? More than once Ramiro was on the verge of asking if anyone in the Commune knew of this Santiago guy, but he didn't. His only reason for not doing so was that he trusted in his comrades less than in the man who clearly lied to him day and night: he could not erase the unfortunate episode with the lady from Vallecas from his memory, he questioned the moral implications of his militancy and the seriousness of his work after his conversations with Lidia, he tolerated less and less what he interpreted on Carmen's part as bullshit lacking in empathy. He sometimes thought, and he told Santiago, that this form of activism – that did not yield results – was a naive way of passing the time, an unpragmatic theatrical performance. He asked Santiago if he knew the women from the church and he had only good things to say about them.

An image that frequently reappeared in Ramiro's mind was Santiago's house with its hallway full of closed doors. Sometimes it seemed to him that nothing had changed since that first moment, that everything was still exactly the same, and that this was how both suspicion and secrecy could be represented: an apartment full of locks and someone who wanted to open them all to offer tenderness and a cup of coffee. Although perhaps things had changed, now it was like living in rooms with false walls and secret passages, existing between overlapping spaces, or finding oneself trapped in anything that could serve the function of a mirror. If Santiago now emptied his pantry, exhibited it in front of him, stripped it of his worms, any metaphorical interpretation of reality could never be enough, every simile would hide a mountain of unanswered shadows. Like other things, one chose to live with a secret. Little by little, Ramiro emptied the container with the larvae, poured the white vinegar down the drain, holding the creatures back carefully, separating them with the same toothpicks that he had used as a rod and a net. Dumping all the bodies in the bin and tying the bag shut, he discovered Santiago absorbed, staring into space and smoking a cigarette. Feeling observed, Santiago took out the Sanytol and scrubbed each of the surfaces on which the worms could have passed. They did not look at each other: only the clock and its hands remained, swinging – back and forth like the sponge – in circular movements. They would have stopped time if stopping it was something they could afford.

PART FOUR:
WRATH

Some preliminary reflections. Big social transformations, as it should have been made clear by now, have always been physical transformations, material transformations that take place in our immediate surroundings. Believe the bourgeois who, at just a glance, understood how much of the land they observed could belong to them; believe the landowner who speculated with resources that he even – shamelessly – went so far as to call *futures*. Every great conquest has rearranged the world in exactly the same way Soviet set designers rearranged representation. Conquest is but a series of wheels, gears, ladders, and bridges that give way to the enormous machine of things – it reflects what, in this world of things, only has space within the impossible. Imperialism is a policy of expansion, domination, and the re-appropriation of what belongs to others, but it is just one policy among many: everything that has anything to do with space is, first and foremost, a manifestation of desire, a manifestation that relentlessly seizes, that always aspires to something more, that requires an almost infinite presence in the world through implantation or conquest. Around a single space, people live in similar ways, share customs, imitate each other, imagine futures with buildings and projects that always emerge from similar planes. They are brothers, and these sentiments are a case of strict filiation. Within these shared spaces, everything comes from a network of networks, a fine and imperceptible web of work passed down from generation to generation.

Capitalist supremacy is both about the absolute metamorphosis of the battlefield, and also what happens on that battlefield. Capitalism's triumph is another subtle conquest – no longer a spatial conquest, but psychological. Capitalism is a total appropriation of the dopamine-releasing mesolimbic pathway, the limitless eagerness that manages and coordinates every source of desire, relaxation, pleasure, happiness and anguish. The capitalist city, in its ideal world, imposes a life in transit, a life of constant movement on the subject, a life in which he does not think, does not suffer, and does not feel – because he does not have time for any of those things. Capitalism defines the spaces that are dedicated to leisure – both out of mercy and to maximise the possibilities of their regulation – and transforms everything else into intravenous lines. It channels the intravenous lines and controls the drip of serum, it allows those very flows to legislate and prepares everything so that the lines are administered by the very people who suffer from them so that power inhabits them, implants itself in their body, occupies, swells, expands.

But sometimes the story and the names behind it offer resistance. Madrid, in this way, was a capricious city; it would have been convenient to explode a bomb in its centre to get rid of the irrational distribution of its streets. In Barcelona's Raval, where the objective was to renovate it for *regulated* life, there were no qualms about destroying narrow streets and cutting umbilical cords in order to flatten large vacant lots to allow surveillance and control in the form of squares and neighbourhoods devoid of alleyways. Madrid had not yet dared to destroy itself in order to stay alive, had not yet allowed itself to be reborn with rational planning; the question is whether it had not happened for fear of the consequences, or if it was simply the result of inaction. Baron Haussmann alone rebuilt Paris at his whim in the nineteenth century, destroying the dingy and dusty city of alleys and walkways, displacing the working class to the periphery, destroying everything to create, inventing a Paris that had never existed before, putting urbanism in the hands of order and the military: substituting the alleys for large avenues, installing boulevards, preventing insurrection. The great project of the nineteenth century had been to install power and control through the streets, not in them, not with planning or surveillance, but with the streets' own materials, present in the tarmac and cobblestones, present in the trees. There were those who interpreted the Paris Commune as a radical insurrection against that urban authoritarianism. I don't know how much you experienced what happened, and I will never be able to know, but you should understand that none of it would have been possible if the streets of Madrid were different.

The call-out was the most successful to date. The entire crossroad at Calle Princesa was filled with protestors, of which only a small percentage – the manageable – were militant activists from the Castillo or belonged to the sub-group of families they helped. The rest were sympathisers: dangerous, Santiago confirmed, because they could not be controlled. Two paces away were a skin head and an old man who pushed his wife in a wheelchair, assuming that everything would remain within the limits of the law, that everything would be peaceful. Wrapped around the old man's neck like a cloak was a Spanish flag that read 'LONG LIVE SPANISH UNITY!'. A father with a shaved head held up his five-year-old son on his shoulders as a group of youngsters from the Castillo chanted about the right to housing. The father wore one of the official shirts – black, with the turrets of the Castillo printed in white – and the mother watched in a white jumper and a pair of comfortable trousers. Most impressive were the flags that covered the protesters like a quilt, billowing like a protective cloak; red, golden, blue, and black. Francoist symbols, crowns and eagles were absent, but Madrid's symbol, the bear, and the image of its throne and power, the Castillo, were present. On occasion, with total autonomy, the flags referenced international brothers – the Italian tortoise from the Roman renaissance, those from Paris with their symbol of a lambda surrounded by a ring. In the overhead shot, only the flags would be seen, fading and concealing, serving as a hiding place for those present who came from all over the peninsula. The longer flag poles were impressive, wielded and flamed with military prowess. The demonstration's route was brief, but it passed through Gran Vía, and passing though Gran Vía was what mattered. The turnout was so great that anything seemed possible. *Long live Spain! Working class and Spanish, working class and Spanish, working class and Spanish, working class and Spanish, working class and Spanish!* One small group had organised a small drum circle in protest, provoking laughter from some of the activists from the Castillo. For now, everything was limited to a few anti-fascist groups who had come to yell a couple of chants; they knew that the majority were in the simultaneous protest, from which they had not yet heard any news. Others shouted, 'here are the anti-fascists' when they weren't thumping and whacking their pans or shaking their tambourines. The Castillo and their people responded with 'here are the nationalists' as the Captain glared at the ultras who were lifting their arms in a Nazi salute.

Santiago had been tasked with writing the speech that would play in the background of the video they would broadcast, the speech the Captain would sing out when they finally reached the end point of the march, Plaza de Dos de Mayo.

I am sure you leave your house in a rush every morning. You run for the bus, you run to class, you run to your internship, you run to the office: your only worry in that precise moment is not being late. That your boss doesn't give you a dressing down for arriving five minutes late.

On such occasions he didn't work alone: the Captain imposed her presence and they negotiated each word carefully. Santiago had meticulously studied the transition from the second-person singular to the first-person plural, but he didn't succeed in imposing it at the moment he would have chosen. The Captain insisted that the repetitions sounded better than they appeared in writing and he ended up conceding to her. The most important thing was to suggest a situation of almost universal misery in which an entire target audience could recognise itself.

And what if you asked yourself, why, what for? You are just one more cog, easily substituted for someone more obedient, more efficient in all this precariousness, in this modern form of exploitation. When have you ever run to fight for your rights? How many times have you run to fight for your dignity? That dignity is something you can't wait five more minutes for.

Maybe you live on your knees: you believe it's the only way to survive. But surviving on your knees is to die alive, to forget who you are and why you are here. Think of the river of blood and sweat that flowed in the name of your dignity yesterday. Think of the men and women who gave their lives so this country could be free and sovereign. The thought of being late to work never crossed their minds. They thought about dignity, about your dignity.

Think of the sacrifices that our fathers and grandfathers made to protect the rights that today you are losing: health care, pensions, work contracts, housing, education. Respect, dignity, and honour. They decided to wake up and not wait five more minutes: they knew that it was always now or never. Today, you decide.

The key was that of ambiguity, almost confusion, but it would not be effective if it were not a matter of sincere ambiguity, of well-measured and studied confusion. The criticism of 'modern exploitation' was not virtue signalling, but Santiago's discursive victory. Once he had managed to slip in that component, the rest flowed effortlessly and he easily extracted the words that followed from within himself. Hope burrowed itself in the hearts of those who heard the message: there was an alternative to death. There was an option that was not only dignified, but noble, honourable; it represented values, continued a tradition, came from a long lineage, and was directly related to the history of this country. And thanks to that option I became we. The distance between the participant and that life came down to a matter of choice: you could have everything you wanted if you only wanted it enough.

It is clear: the dignity of our people cannot be sold, nor is it given away. Dignity is not traded, because dignity is not demolished, or burned, or locked up. We must put an end to a system in which even air is traded on the stock market: these are years in which fairytale castles in the sky have risen in value. Years of misery. And what if we realised that we don't need the IBEX 35 to exist? What if we realised who we really were, a people, a history, overcoming the ruins of this world together?

This new discursive mutation emerged from the time that his rhetoric had spent maturing. In this type of message, well focused on specific audiences and with recurring keywords that were easily picked up by online algorithms, the sermon had eliminated all traces of unwanted negativity. Other messages, aimed at other audiences, would insist on issues such as immigration and refugees, and their gang rapes, their violence, their robberies, or their criminality. The Castillo, on the other hand, would confirm that in no case was it a question of hate, but a question of order, and that the important thing had never been aversion to others, that there was no animosity towards outsiders, no unwholesome feelings, no feelings attached to rancour or sin; there was only an acknowledgment of statistical truths, a will to protect one's own, to get rid of the knots and beasts encircling one's own, to tear the fairytale castles out of the sky, to put an end to so many years of misery. They would conquer the power that could penetrate the cells of an entire Society, permeate everything, turn everything into a territory of conquest: overcome the ruins of this world by establishing themselves in them. Whoever could penetrate the cells of an entire society, permeate everything, turn everything into a territory of conquest, would conquer power. Santiago would overcome the ruins of this world by establishing himself in them.

Our people will place those who speculated, gambled, and mortgaged the dreams of an entire country in the unemployment line. If they fill their pockets thanks to the suffering of our people, we will fill the streets and squares shouting our names and theirs, remembering who we were, who we are and who they are, fighting for the memory of those who could not see their dreams come true. Fighting for justice, fighting for dignity: for those who are yet to come and who will never see theirs if we don't make a great effort now.

Here was the instrumental piece: the use of revenge and anger, taking advantage of the seductive force of the ruins, the horrors, the crimes, the chaos of a total war, to endure in a movement, a movement of constant response. It was fundamental to not only affirmatively shout 'our names', but to also point to the heads that were to be decapitated, to not only remind them of those who 'will fill the squares' and play with the contemporary political unconscious, to not only remind them of who they were, but to establish them as something that would last long into the future, to make their resistance known, to make them believe in themselves as a clenched fist and an executor. Santiago thought about the words he had prepared and accepted that the day of his conquest had finally arrived. The baton was his and no one could take it away from him.

A better country is still possible, we can still win, we can still be everything they try to steal from us, we can still be the sword and shield of our dreams.

The anti-fascist protest was starting to make its way down the Paseo del Prado. Ramiro saw joy in the faces of the people that glanced at the slogans and the multitude of flags: pink, purple, republican, from the Castilian independence movement, rainbow, red and black, and flags with the official logo of the anti-fascist convocation. The river of people was an endless torrent. A flagpole served as a link to join two comrades who were overseeing the cordon. Vero had collaborated with the organisation, and even Lidia came with a group of friends, assuming that there wouldn't be any kind of altercation, that everything would unfold with the utmost tranquillity.

Santiago assumed that Ramiro knew that there were more anti-fascists, that their attendance was greater, and he imagined him as confident, sure of himself, ready for anything, agile, much more agile than him, a warrior, brave. Ramiro would have liked Santiago to have been by his side, to see what he saw, and he broke free from the others for a moment, taking advantage of a lull to write 'you still have time to come, you can take line one and we can meet here, I wish you were here. I think things will stay calm, there won't be any madness, you could come and you wouldn't have to run, there's no danger, I don't think the police want to get involved today.' Santiago's phone didn't receive the messages. Ramiro imagined that he had turned it off so to be able to concentrate on studying for the government exams. He went back to join his two comrades as they marched slowly. It took him a while to realise that the atmosphere among the organisers had turned, they seemed to have spotted someone suspicious on the opposite flank and expelled him from the demonstration. A few metres away, a few girls insisted that their block was non-mixed, courteously asking a boy to move away or join another.

Santiago asked the Captain when they were going to start the march. The minutes they had delayed for were accumulating, he told her. He didn't know what the reason for this could be; the counterdemonstration must have already left. The Captain dismissed the matter and said that they wouldn't cross paths anyway, that their route was very short, that they were waiting for the arrival of a good handful of activists who had been delayed. They couldn't leave without them, because then the sections would be completely separated from each other. She smiled and asked him for his confidence. *We're the ones who are least interested in seeing this all get out of hand, Santi, you said it yourself, very clearly: we fear that we have to convey that we're a peaceful organisation, that we don't appear as violent, that we don't under any circumstances look like a gang of exasperated radicals who just go around looking for a fight. Relax and enjoy yourself.*

Time continued to pass until the demonstration finally decided to move forward at a snail's pace. Slowly, they penetrated Gran Vía from Plaza de España. The circulation of traffic moving around the plaza had been blocked by the police who guarded the protesters and they exchanged a few nervous words with the organisation and the Captain. Santiago had met with the Captain on numerous occasions, he had prepared all the initial plans and organised all of the legal authorisations, but he had not participated in any of the decisive meetings that decided on the development of the demonstration. *It's not your field, it's not your speciality*, she repeated, *you're almost always more useful to us with words than you are with images, and you know their effects. This is so different.* Santiago bit his lip, the inside of his mouth, chewed at his flesh. He was suspicious. He calmed down when he saw the children, the prams, the families, the elderly.

But the two large groups did meet in the middle of Gran Vía, just at the point where the street veered slightly left, leaving behind the Santo Domingo metro station. Santiago had guessed correctly: the anti-fascist demonstration seemed much more crowded. What's more, for some reason, his was emptying out with small gradual desertions, a whole trickle that calmly disappeared and scattered out towards Silva, Libreros, Tudescos and the rest of the contiguous streets that went north. Face to face, with a ridiculous police unit keeping their distance and riot vans in the middle, silence set in. For a moment, there were no shouts, no one spoke, no one proclaimed anything, nothing moved. Time held its breath. Many of those remaining in Santiago's bloc were taking out, one after the other, masks and canisters of easily recognisable light blue smoke: they were the same ones that had appeared in the promotional videos that he edited and uploaded to the Castillo's official channel. About five or six columns of black smoke rose, piercing the mass like spears. Little by little, more and more appeared, and seeing became difficult. The anti-fascist bloc did not know, wrapped up in the ambiguity that anticipated the storm, if everything was mere provocation or if the worst was to come. Rain had been announced for the whole week but today it was sunny, the sky pristine. They chanted, making an effort to remain calm and keep their form, 'here are the anti-fascists'. At the cordon Ramiro and the others began to circulate the message that the sympathisers and the most vulnerable from the group should go back to the rear of the procession in case there was any altercation or attack, be it 'from the fascists' or 'from their henchmen', their dogs, their pets, their minions: the police. Then blue columns of smoke sprouted up among the vanguard of the anti-fascist demonstration, the cordon unravelled, some screams were heard, and small balls of smoke rolled across the anti-fascist bloc, almost reaching the Palacio de la Prensa. The riot police battened their shields and braced their helmets. Then the unthinkable happened: a Molotov cocktail hit the police van, the flammable liquid spread, and the car started to burn with an officer inside. A few of his colleagues ran to get him out, help him, but the man burned with his helmet still on, and his visor blew out. Who had thrown it? Where did it come from? The trajectory pointed to the periphery of the anti-fascist demonstration, but such an explanation would not make sense. By the time they had realised that the origin was an infiltrator, it was already too late. Suddenly the police found themselves in the middle of a flock of hooligans that ploughed from one side of Gran Vía to the other with machetes and clenched fists. Thanks to a false attack, a civil war had started in the centre of Madrid.

Santiago looked for the Captain but couldn't find her anywhere. The image of the burning man horrified him. In the absence of the Captain, and with reams of people leaving the march little by little, the loose frays, the suppuration, in the total absence of families and the homeless that at the beginning were on the frontline, he couldn't stop thinking about who it had been, who had started it all, if it had been them. He was almost motionless as the rest of them ran and pushed back towards the police and the anti-fascists. Chaos installed itself from within and on both sides of Santiago the crowd surged like a stampede.

He watched the maelstrom that was Callao, two minutes and three wrong moves away from becoming a blood bath. He had convinced himself, when elaborating the speech, that their victory was close: he had repeated to himself over and over again that all the times he had dreamt that things were getting out of hand had been nothing more than nightmares, feverish delusions, a fear of failing that had been ignored and that he could have managed better with a little more discipline. He had come to believe that he could prevail over brute force and methods that he presupposed 'natural' to the organisation. The idea that the Captain had betrayed him and got involved with the adrenaline almost made his stomach, his oesophagus, even his larynx twist and turn. The idea that this plan was drawn up by Alejandro when he found out about the intentions of the anti-fascists – when he read that fateful message that he saw on the networks, the message spread by Ramiro that 'fascists are stopped by breaking their legs' – was unbearable. He remained motionless and mute in the midst of the screams. As a sad helpless spectator, he watched how the broken glass of the Starbucks window fell. He envisioned all the images that he always fantasised about and that he could never crystalise. Chairs flew between protesters and it seemed that his people were going on the offensive, that they were ahead. He thought of Ramiro. He wondered where Ramiro was, if he was ok. Coughing from the smoke that covered everything, he put on his mask and ran.

He thought that if he could manage to get to Miguel Moya and reach Plaza de la Luna from there, making his way towards the north through those narrow streets, that maybe he could get to safety, find the Captain again, ask her for some answers. He slipped through the fire and the passers-by who were fleeing as the shops closed their doors on them; some had found refuge in the underground parking. It was too late when he realised there was a police station in Plaza de la Luna that he was running straight towards with a blue mask covering his face. He thought about taking it off, but the police were already coming down the street. He turned around and ran and could hear that they were following him, he ran like he had never run before in his life. Now he wasn't heading down Miguel Moya, but had instead turned onto the adjacent Tudescos and was going back on himself: towards Gran Vía, the heart of the battle. Someone had broken the screens outside the Capitol Cinema, but he was still able to make out what they were showing, and the banality of it fell flat: *Captain America 3: Civil War*, *Pride and Prejudice*, and *Zombies*. The hotel had blocked its doors as people took photographs and recorded videos from balconies and windows. Worried that his face would end up appearing in one of the videos, he was thankful for the mask. The electronic billboards in Callao dazzled between the fumes and the clouds of smoke. For now, the battle was concentrated on Gran Vía and in Plaza de Callao, and hadn't turned back down towards Santo Domingo. Some hooded men without masks, who didn't have anything to do with either group, broke the windows of a few shops and entered to sack them. An uber overturned amid the ruckus, a traffic light harmlessly fell in the middle of the zebra crossing, and from Miguel Moya one, two, three police cars descended. The pursuit receded and the crusade moved away from the central artery of Gran Vía to return the side streets; a few anti-fascists were chasing those from some of the other factions who were trying to flee in the direction of Noviciado – the logic was to put Gran Vía behind them – as a kiosk burned in front of the twenty-four-hour tobacconist.

Without knowing how, or by what means, Santiago arrived in Plaza Conde de Toreno in one piece. Someone threw an empty bottle at one of the riot vans, but the throw failed and hit the floor as those who had launched it ran to hide behind the lift down to the metro. The two bars on the square had closed their doors and pulled down the metal shutters; some civilians sheltered inside as two of the containers in the plaza burned. As the conflict was triangular, and nobody knew very well which one of those the third group, the police, favoured, everyone was throwing whatever they could get their hands on past the fire, running backwards and returning forwards and taking advantage of the narrow streets to avoid crossing paths. It wasn't Paris, the practice of *nasse* had still not spread through Spain enough to justify using it as an adopted term – the one chosen would be *police kettling* – although similar models had been used in previous mobilisations: police tactics consisting of isolating a group of protesters, enclosing them, holding them in a space for a long period of time, and leading the procession to a well-chosen end point to, at least in France, suffocate them with tear gas and break them up. The police had also not yet adopted water cannons or other powerful technologies of control and repression. A police presence as God intended would have involved the deployment of the anti-terrorist unit, a helicopter flying through the skies like a kite, even a tank and jets.

How could they have allowed this? How could they have been so negligent? The deployment organised by the Government Delegation had been so small, Santiago thought, that everything that was happening could only be classified as a direct consequence of abandonment: the government – the power – had abandoned the city to violence. He was fully aware that no type of power withdrew like this if it was not with the intention of achieving something greater, but he failed to recognise any interests that were capable of explaining why they had stepped back to fan the flame. At another time he would have thought of an electoral turnaround, of small spurious and banal interests, the will to win a few votes by establishing themselves as the force that maintained order in the face of chaos proposed by others. That didn't seem like it was what mattered today. No, this negligence was simply a mechanism through which the naïve were allowed to dream of the impossible for a while.

The chaos in this area was the result of the dispersion of a few anti-fascist groups, independent of each other, who had been able to corner off a few of the remaining streets. The other side still held Plaza del Conde de Toreno. The anti-fascists seemed to have control of the streets of Reyes and Álamo, though after another police van had sped through without stopping, reinforcements appeared from the north down Calle Amaniel: a horde of hooded hooligans ran in and dispersed throughout the area, forcing the anti-fascists to back off. Air gun shots were heard. Those on the defence tried to entrench themselves in Calle Álamo, but they were not aware that the ultras' only interest was to continue onto Calle Reyes. The hooded figures came across a boy looking for his group on Calle Álamo, and they shoved him, threw him to the ground, and started kicking him until he lost consciousness. They argued about what to do. Almost mocking him, they approached the entrance to Calle Reyes with the body, cadaverous, and propped it up in front of the bins that had been piled up like a barricade. The fire in the containers was still alive. They abandoned the body and someone from his side ran for him. Then, along with Santiago, the ultras moved past the bins, taking advantage of the fact that the anti-fascist group had left their post to help their comrade. They ran all the way to Calle San Bernardo, almost reaching the Noviciado metro. They found smoke and more police vans, but a huge blaze separated them from where the street intersected with Calle Manzana, where they assumed that the anti-fascists remained, and where a fire truck had appeared. One of the riot vans left the two groups alone on Calle San Bernardo. They knew that if they continued to regain territory, their escape to the north would be much easier. They imagined that the enemy had control over Mostenses, the central nucleus of Gran Vía, and the extensions towards Tribunal, Bilbao, and Alonso Martínez. The objective, as victory was always relative, was to reach the northeast without suffering defeat.

The flow led Santiago to where Calle del Pez intersected with Calle Cruz Verde. The bookshop was closed, the tobacconist too. The ground cracked open, and a new barricade rose from the surface; Santiago crouched down and hid behind it. He looked up for a moment, clutching the bin, and came up against Alejandro who effortlessly took over the space, his rugged features hidden by a mask that matched his own.

'This was your idea, you stupid, arrogant bastard.'

'Mate, Santiago! How are you? Extremities intact? Are your little arms alright or will you be stiff tomorrow?

'Go fuck yourself.'

'There'll be time for that later. Do you see this beauty around us? Or hear it? Tune in any of your senses: it's everywhere. If I were you, I would settle down very comfortably and enjoy the spectacle. Do you know the only thing I regret? That it was impossible to get to Palacio de Cibeles or blow out the top of the skyscrapers on Gran Vía. Imagine if we had the means to broadcast all of this ourselves, and not have to deal with zillions of teenagers recording live videos from their phones! But you know the good thing? Everything happens step by step, little by little, like the tortoise and the hare: no rush. Strap in, Santiago, there are some bends in the road ahead.'

'Do you not realise the shit you've started?'

'We all wanted this, we all participated.'

'And what about what the Captain said? Let them be the group of organised violence, distance ourselves, make ourselves the image of justice?'

'What you said through the Captain, you mean? Your little ideas, deployed like a ventriloquist? We had other images in our minds. Your words have only helped us accumulate anger and translate it.'

Alejandro had changed his mind about something, but Santiago didn't know what. There was something in Santiago that was pre-emptively devastated, but Alejandro was happy, he was happy, he was radiant, he raised his arms and waved them like a celebrity turning up in the middle of the party with drinks and invitations for everyone, jumping the line, entering via the red carpet, blowing kisses, waving to everyone. War was no longer a nuisance to him: once things had been set into motion, once the space had been transformed by the activity that was present, Madrid had turned into a huge party. They headed down the street, far from the territorial distributions that trapped them just a few moments ago, Alejandro agilely buffeting his heavy body between the fire and the bins. All the bodies moved to the beat like shadows surrounded by embers and ashes and screams and lights that snuck in as they moved in silence. For a moment, Santiago could have sworn that he could hear music, that the towers were preparing to fall one after the other in his wake. The sirens set a rhythm accompanied by the coughing from the smoke, and the systematic rotation of the police cars' blue lights in alternation with the fire generated the flashes. The people had multiplied, a calling effect; among everything else he could still hear pistol shots. The police had sent down more patrols and now they really were trying to retain people, but they had, of course, arrived too late. They were obliged to act, Santiago supposed: they couldn't let the city burn without lifting their fingers just a little.

Once, he had heard Alejandro tell a story. He was really drunk after an assembly in the Castillo, and he took on a trembling tone, suffering from the slight imbalances that the inner ear suffered when too much alcohol had been consumed. He towered over everyone like a great building on the verge of collapsing. *On the outskirts of Paris, in 2005*, Alejandro recounted, *two guys died, two kids, because of a police mistake: they were trying to run from a stop and search. What happened next was that those populations unleashed like beasts. The French State had to mobilise more than eleven thousand police officers every day. More than ten thousand cars and hundreds of public and private buildings were burned. In a single night, more than seven hundred people were imprisoned and several thousand were arrested.*

The clashes lasted for weeks. Weeks with the world in suspense, the city burning, police action exposing itself in the most primal, savage way. Weeks in which a people rejected the executors of the law, considering them and it immoral. They are beasts. We cannot trust them, they react like this because they do not know how to react in any other way. The police killed one of theirs and they did not want to make amends, debate, compromise: no, what they wanted to do was burn a fucking car, they wanted revenge. Because it was the only way they knew how to act. If you try to control them too much, if they feel that the hand around their neck is too tight, suffocating, they explode, they consider it unwarranted. They're still angry, but they lack strength, they talk about institutional racism, they say that all the police are evil, sons of bitches. They don't know what they're doing, I'm telling you, but they continue to do it anyway. If another of their own dies, they will burn the streets again. Because this emotion burns in individuals and from their ashes arise the collective, the mob, the animal. The strength of that emotion is electric: knowing that you will not die in vain, knowing that you are the victim of injustice. Understand that there is no option: you can only respond to the war proclaimed by the other through war. Knowing that violence is condemnable, and... yes, I might laugh when I say it... but that it is also understandable. Be beasts. Accept the force. Understand that violence only ends with violence. And resist this reign of death by lording our control over it.

Santiago was not hallucinating: someone on Gran Vía was in fact carrying an enormous loudspeaker and a great silent procession came up from Calle Preciados, lined with trees releasing the scent of jacaranda. The flows of people in one direction and another were so frequent and repetitive that it was already possible to ignore them: the world as he knew it disappeared as rhythm took shape and vibrations returned to reconfigure every cell of everything present. Santiago no longer knew what he saw, or how. From what should have just been a mere confrontation between two groups that hated each other, Alejandro had managed to ring the bell of death. He wondered what united all these people who wanted to destroy the city and destroy their enemies, he wondered what could be heard beneath the roar, who spoke and who answered, who would give the order to stop the voice. Didn't he also have reasons to defend the fire? He did, and he recognised that his anger could be anyone's. The sweet scent of jacaranda gave way to the stench of rubbish pouring from the bins, and he imagined the tragic Molotov cocktail crashing against a bin lorry, though the image didn't pain him. He realised something else: the only reason he didn't also condemn the world to flames was because now he did have something that he couldn't bear to lose. And then, in the distance, he saw Ramiro, recognisable beneath the black hood and the scarf that covered his mouth: he would have recognised that person behind any body, hidden in the depths of any pair of eyes. He stayed still until he was certain that he had not been seen, and then he ran back down Gran Vía and turned onto Calle San Bernardo, almost brushing the side of a police motorcycle. He was learning how to handle the storm, the lights, the dance, the party. No longer knowing where anyone was or even what to do – just run? – he realised that his objective had once been to reach the Captain. And he said goodbye to the centre of a burning Madrid with a quick glance: others would wage that war, he thought, he knew it was no longer his.

I don't want to get to what is to come. I could stop the story here, leave the fire as the last image, not continue. But you already know what comes next. I keep wondering what you saw, how you reacted, what you thought of those who wanted to convert so much cement, concrete, brick, and mortar into fuel, to paint the neighbourhoods with broken glass. Up to here, the images I have are blurred, a mixture of what I saw and what I later watched on the news. I was haunted by a constant and obsessive reasoning of the events, an attempt to sound out opinion, short videos, chases, what almost seemed like murders: all the chaos that I've outlined here. What was going through your head while all this was happening? You thought of coming to beat up my lot, didn't you? Was that your intention? I could never believe that as even if you had been able to, you wouldn't have been capable of it. You're not like that. I would have liked to blow Alejandro's head off, but I was not capable: I'm not like that. I find it hard to put the images that follow into words, they escape from between my fingers like parasites and cover my hands with sores and holes but, if anything, I will try to translate them for you, convert them into a lexicon and a grammar, break their essence. It will never be the same. These words won't be able to scare you as much as I did, the panic will be completely absent from your mind, and in my story there will be no anguish, I will be completely alone before the immensity of the world. Can we go back to sweeter images? I know that there are images that are worse still than the ones that are to come now, and I understand that I will have to study them carefully, because they continue to invade me, sneaking in like intruders, but I would like so much to be able to go back to sweeter images, images that are as tender as we could be.

Santiago was cornered on Calle de la Palma, just before it arrived at Plaza del Dos de Mayo. He had no way of escaping if he went towards the parallel Calle San Vincente Ferrer, because there was a group of anti-fascists there. Two of them were chasing him and one disappeared down another street while the other approached him. Santiago did not have enough strength to resist and ended up against the wall. He recognised his scent. The boy pulled down his light blue mask. From the second their eyes met he knew it was Ramiro. They didn't speak. Ramiro threw him against the wall, immediately ripped off his mask and left him lying on the ground as he ran down the street.

Anticipating that the rope was about to break did not lessen the fall: that all of Madrid was in flames did not matter so much to him in this moment. He was more aware than ever of the brittle threads that he himself had irresponsibly pulled tighter and tighter. He abandoned any plans to search for the Captain. His right arm hurt: it was hit when he was pushed by Ramiro, all his muscles were still tense, and he thought he had pulled his calf. Leaving the pieces of his mask on the ground, he headed towards Tribunal metro station. He was dying of rage and so preferred to hold back his emotions instead beginning to plan what he was going to do tomorrow, and the day after, and the day after.

Would he burn too? Was this disaster beyond hope, had everything lost all meaning? The Captain would have no other option but to disassociate herself from Alejandro, declare that these riots were never her intention, lie until it was clear that everything was the result of a violent anti-fascist who had infiltrated the Castillo, invent an alibi and distance herself from all the groups with whom she had demonstrated, make it clear that her organisation never wanted anything like this to happen, detach herself from the facts and condemn the violence, condemn all violence. At first, he thought he would be there when it was time to write the words. He would always be there, like her faithful dog: he had nothing else left.

But then he thought again and considered that he wanted to leave, to disassociate himself from the Castillo, to do something else with his life, to become aware of the brittle threads that the others had pulled: his ambition was too great, his failure was embodied throughout the city, his failure was the fire that consumed everything, his failure was putrefaction, the world that burned in the air, the parasites that had won the game. He had cast aside the images but now he didn't believe in words either. Why go back to the Castillo if he would only see his leader shifting, balancing the scales to contain one and the other, tainting the faint-hearted and brutalising the already brutalised? He couldn't believe this dirty game, this defeat. He looked at the lights, and he thought that Madrid was no longer the kingdom of heaven that he imagined it could be, he thought about how it had never even been close but was rather an incarnation of hell, a great tomb, the biggest necropolis in history. He imagined the policeman burning and wanted someone to tie Alejandro's hands, subdue him, handcuff him.

Contempt returned as the night went on. In what remains of these memories I recognise myself: I was already aware then of having lost you. I imagined the policeman on fire, and I wanted someone to tie Alejandro's hands, subdue him, handcuff him. I couldn't believe this dirty game, this defeat. I looked at the lights. I cast aside the images but I didn't believe in words either. I didn't take the metro but sat on a bench in front of San Ildefonso church and observed its abominable colour with horror, the way it had been abandoned, its star, its arbitrary clock, its bells, its painting, the graffiti. A boy ran by being chased by three other people; I was indifferent. I only looked when I thought, for a moment, that the prey could be you. The boy was not similar to you in any way, neither in his eyes nor his form, neither in his body nor his mannerisms. I swore I would recognise you anywhere and there was no similarity to you there, not a trace: I returned to my church. I was indifferent to the Madrid that was burning, it was banal, like all the fires caused by arsonists, and it could burn six more nights without me lifting a finger to stop it. When it seemed that things had calmed down, I got up, walked down the street towards Tribunal and ended up going into a bar without thinking. I found a seat at the back and I drank, and I continued to gaze at the world with contempt. My eyes were black, my sockets irrigated with salt water, black water on a dark night, my pupils submerged in an iris of boiling water. Everyone was mired in kerosene and took on the shapes of shadows, transforming into silhouettes or ghosts, or stains, hipster stains, posh stains, smug stains, full stains, puffed up with themselves, and I was surrounded by so many happy, radiant young people, so ignorant to what had happened just a moment ago. They were looking at images of the demonstration and the riot on their phones, they were attempting to find a topic of conversation or the perfect shot – so stupid, they had photographs that were so perfect, so pretentious, so typical of arseholes. They were untouchable, from another planet, without weak points, invulnerable to the serious. They were frivolous chameleons, capable of going to bed as something and waking up as its opposite, savers, and lovers of waste, without the need for money, without the need for education. They were soulless, lifeless but apparently happy, absorbed, exhausted, scavengers of the joy of others. They had white eyes, their sockets irrigated with foam or saline solution, always living in toxic rose sunsets, rose, rose like death, rose like rose roses.

I knew that the worst was to come; I already knew it then.

PART FIVE: PRIDE

Now you know we've reached the days I don't want to remember. I got out of that night unscathed, although I don't quite know if unscathed is the right word. I remember having written you a message explaining how sorry I was, begging you to forgive me. I expressed all my fears so you could understand how I had been tormented by the certainty that I would lose you as soon as you really got to know me. I think a lot about who you would talk to, who you would tell, the reaction of your roommates, how I never gave you your keys back. Was it a sign of trust that you never asked for them? Was it as if you were admitting that approaching you was impossible, was it you saying that no more words would be shared between the two of us? At the same time were you accepting that I was not a threat in any way? Did you assume that what we had had was real? Should I thank you?

Maybe they didn't believe you. They must have thought it was a joke at first: a communist falls in love with a fascist, I'm sure you used that word, *fascist*. You probably said almost without believing it that you had a fascist boyfriend, that I had cheated on you because all this time I had been one of those, one of the bad guys, one of the enemy. You would only have had to investigate a little more, dig a little deeper, ask around to see who knew this Santiago guy. Maybe you already knew and that's why you didn't. I think about that, I really do, sometimes I think that you knew all along and you kept quiet until I found out by force that you knew who I was, I can't find any other explanation. I covered my back and sometimes I almost disappeared, but I couldn't make myself invisible - someone should have told you everything, someone should have recognised me. Everything should have been revealed at another time, when our trenches were not facing each other, our comrades protecting us from the crossfire.

I have thought so many times about what you might ask me should we ever exchange words again, little words between us both. Of course, I would have liked to communicate with you in other ways but, at some point, we would have had to push those feelings back down and reduce ourselves to language. But how could that have ever been possible, and how silly does it sound when I say it like that, that I would ignore what you were so that our story could live on? I guess I had always allowed myself little contradictions. You never asked me to choose, and I would not have dared; I was aware that you were my purpose, and the Castillo was just a force of habit, but I knew that you would see things a different way. Now it was my turn to be the idiot who wanted more. I didn't want to love anyone, and until you I didn't know that I was capable of doing so: I didn't love my father, and no one can love absence, I supposed for a while that those scraps were enough to mutilate me for life, to render me loveless, to make me an emotional cripple, an abominable monster. Then you arrived and it was incomprehensible, your whole body invited tenderness. At first, I couldn't tolerate it, I thought that if I tried to love you, I would be the one to die, and you would have to bear the full weight of my corpse in your arms.

'Like a little swallow, with broken wings.' That's how Leonida Bongiorno put his first impression of Edda Ciano into words. They were like us, equally stupid, our ancestors. Edda, Mussolini's daughter and head of the section of the Italian Communist Party on the largest island of the Aeolian archipelago, a paradise on earth formed from God's drops of divine greatness left here for us to inhabit. Leonida, the son of Eduardu Bongiorno, founder of the Lipari Socialist Labour Movement. They talked non-stop, like us, in the Timparozzo house, and he recited verses from the Odyssey by heart while she drank up his words. They went to the beach, they bathed, they were happy.

If you affect it, open ear allow
To try their motion; but presume not so
To trust your judgement, when your senses go
So loose about you, but give straight command
To all your men, to bind you foot and hand
Sure to the mast, that you may safe approve
How strong in instigation to their love
Their rapting tunes are. If so much they move,
That, spite of all your reason, your will stands
To be enfranchis'd both of feet and hands,
Charge all your men before to slight your charge
And rest so far from fearing to enlarge
That much more sure they bind you. When your friends
Have outsail'd these, the danger that transcends
Rests not in any council to prevent,
Unless your own mind finds the tract and bent
Of the way that avoids it. I can say
That in your course there lies a twofold way,
The right of which your own, taught, present wit,
And grace divine must prompt. In general yet
Let this inform you: near these Sirens' shore
Move two steep rocks, at whose feet lie and roar
The black sea's cruel billows; the bless'd gods
Call them the Rovers. Their abhorr'd abodes
No bird can pass – no, not the doves, whose fear
Sir Jove so loves that they are said to bear
Ambrosia to him, can their ravine 'scape,
But one of them falls ever to the rape
Of those sly rocks; yet Jove another still
Adds to the rest, that so may ever fill
The sacred number. Never ship could shun
The nimble peril wing'd there, but did run,

With all her bulk, and bodies of her men,
To utter ruin. For the seas retain
Not only their outrageous testure there,
But fierce assistants of particular fear
And supernatural mischief they expire,
And those are whirlwinds of devouring fire
Whisking about still. Th' Argive ship alone,
Which bore the care of all men, got her gone,
Come from Areta. Yet perhaps ev'n she
Had wrack'd at those rocks, if the deity
That lies by Jove's side, had not lent her hand
To their transmission, since the man that mann'd
In chief that voyage, she in chief did love.*

You never responded to my messages. I came and went from my house, alone, and never even dared to pass in front of yours for fear that you would see me and that there would be no love left in your eyes. I stole my father's change and gleaned the cheapest bars in Madrid, cursing the hours and cursing poverty, getting drunk among others' cries and bad smells, accepting banal and tedious conversations, observing how the entire city suffocated itself as it implored that what happened days before could not happen again, never, never. There were no protests that prolonged the hell of our farewell. The government decreed a curfew for the capital, without the need to extend it to the provinces. The Government Delegate had to resign and a legal process was started against her for negligence (she was eventually acquitted). Army patrols were deployed to maintain order in the streets. I drank until it was time to go home, when the military appeared and beat the windows of the premises as a threat. Sometimes by force of habit, some landlord took pity on me, closed the metal shutters, and invited me to one more, now clandestine, round.

* Homer, *The Odyssey*, tr. George Chapman, Wordsworth Editions, 2000, pp.646-647..

The landlord cut our lines of cocaine – which we never bought ourselves – on the bar. The days passed as the fog passes and each one was the same as the previous; I couldn't recall a single conversation from that time, because I only remember my pain: my memory begins and ends there.

I was weak, like someone who was aware that they were going to die soon and understood that the best way to enjoy the few days they had left was to not do much, resign themselves to fate, embody the wait. I didn't answer any phone calls, I didn't look at any of the group discussions, I ignored all my messages, I didn't attend any meetings. I didn't want to see anyone who might recognise me, I didn't want to be with anyone who knew my identity. In my heart, little by little, the fury – that with you I had left to one side – was installing itself again, resentment was accumulating like plaque in my arteries. If it was possible to die of rage, I would have died; if anger could make a body explode, mine would have exploded. I had grown used to the touch of your body at night and so felt alone, and without tracing your skin I could not sleep. Unsettled, I tossed and turned in bed at night, listening over and over again to the sound of the bin lorries. I spent the days waiting for the nights and in what was left of the night I would hold out until the day came, trying sometimes to possess or abuse your memory, to get closer to you by simply thinking of you. I thought, crazed, that I could talk to you just by trying, that you would listen to my words if I shouted them loudly enough as, delirious, I spoke to myself and scratched the walls as if trying to tear the wallpaper off and find you waiting behind it. I can't tell you how many days I spent like this.

What comes now is what I can best allow myself to imagine. How curious are images, how they provoke, induce vomiting, nausea: the ones that stay with us longest have always been those that in one way or another are related to violence. I don't know if I wanted to perpetrate it, if I wished it or if it simply came to me – like a child making a wish before a shooting star, only to later regret that some capricious god had decided to grant it to him. I finally conjured up the product of all the images that I had dreamed of. I know I take detours and that I twist and turn, but I am not ready to finish. Not in this way.

I will repeat myself: I felt alone and yet, as I knew that your body was irreplaceable, it was impossible to go to the first available piece of meat and extract a few drops of comfort from it. I came to hate you for that, for spoiling me, for making me your little spoiled brat, for giving me things that I never should have gotten used to. Who the hell did you think you were and what the hell did you do to me? Eventually I was aware that I needed a body; I found out that you had blocked me, and I was willing to destroy myself with the first person who contacted me. I wanted them to exterminate me, to turn me into a demolished building, a wasteland, to wipe out all traces of tenderness, to teach me again what my place was, what it always had been, and always would be. Where were you when I needed all those perversities? I liked to imagine that concealed behind one of the profiles, the fingers that typed were yours, agile, that your silly little wobbly legs were behind the screen, shaking like a gazelle, your little toes massaging your soles in unconscious movement. I liked to think that you would want us to meet again like this, without even seeing each other's eyes, without appreciating each other's faces or touching one and other's contours, to be able to share something that you did not accept the possibility of sharing with me: words. I thought of you looking for mirages, hiding places, shortcuts and detours to find me too, pretending that you had moved away only to reappear. I was like a child that still didn't believe in a ruse created by adults. I later came to realise, with bitterness, that for you I was probably replaceable. And I still hadn't got with anyone on that devil's app, no other body had caught my attention enough, and before all the songs the siren remained immobile, bound with more and more ties. But then I imagined you in the arms of someone who wasn't me, subjugated by someone who wasn't me, with the huge, sharp claw of a man that didn't look like me wrapping around your neck, tighter and tighter, squeezing more and more, making you enjoy yourself as only I did, delighting you in a way that with me hadn't even been a possibility, revelling in a complicity that almost cost me death and that I wouldn't be able to repeat, but that appeared to you in two moments, that manifested itself spontaneously, that appeared because one piece fit with the other and then it was as if someone had chosen and placed everything, as if fortune had decided. I accepted the first message, I gave the guy my address, I was greedy to find a reflection of your sex in the sex of others, thinking that the curve their forms drew in the air would be the same as yours, substituting the image of your face in my mind, falsely feeling – and suspending the corrections – that every part, organ, hole or request belonged to you, would always belong to you.

I should have predicted the only way this was going was down. I was an imbecile, an idiot, deeply stupid, abnormal, a dickhead. I stood outside the door of my building thinking that the miracle would repeat itself, that it would be you again, and as I waited outside and smoked a cigarette, I cursed the misfortune that was now my life. Then a hooded body appeared among the night. Because of its hood I thought it was you, I almost raised my hand as if showing my thirst, I almost started to tremble. He moved closer and closer until he removed his hood, and my blood froze. I hope you can excuse all my lies.

'No way, you've got to be kidding me! This can't be true. Well, well, Santiago! I could have met up with anyone tonight...

and it ended up being you!'

Alejandro's laugh was horrible, scraping, metallic, like a broken doll, or the sound of a premature old man drowning; his body strutted from side to side as he approached me with no more dexterity than just another drunkard. His face flooded with satisfaction, his mouth was gaping open, gums inflamed, tartar accumulating – although you could still see something of his teeth beneath the gingivitis. Still laughing, he lit a cigarette and held one out to me, I took it, a remedy. I tried not to see the aggressiveness in that sinister figure. I pulled back and tried to justify myself.

'*I'm* surprised.'

'Are you a faggot? I knew you were a faggot. I told her you were. She kept saying no, no, I know him well, he's just a bit short with girls. But I knew it!'

'You're the one that opened my...'

'Santiago, I think you already know exactly what's happening, but let me explain, just to make it clear to you: I made a fake profile and messaged a guy way out of my neighbourhood, with the intention of smashing his teeth in. But it's you! ... This couldn't be better!'

'I can explain.'

'What do you have to explain?'

'I sleep with guys, but there are no feelings involved. For me it's just something functional, a way of releasing energy, an exercise to manage my impulses. I know they're not natural impulses, so I subdue them and control them. I only see each guy once, then I block them, I don't see anyone for a second time, it disgusts me to think of involving a complicated concoction of feelings. I don't subscribe in any way to a homosexual life, nor do I justify it, nor do I enjoy suffering from this condition. My agreement with the Castillo's ideas is undeniable. The world vision that we have intoned is still mine. I am still your comrade.'

'Mmhmm! Don't tell me that on top of it all you're ashamed by it. Are you a repentant gay, closeted? Do you even know how to get your arse ready?'

'Desire cannot be controlled. And you know perfectly well that someone can be ashamed by their desire.'

'If you're frustrated, you shoot something, smash something. You, how many fags do you get with a month, Santiago? Do you like them older or younger? Bears or twinks: which one makes you harder? You're a pervert, you know, there's something wrong with you. Oh, the punishments that God has prepared for you lot…'

'Don't kill me.'

'Who spoke about killing? You're getting ahead of yourself. Calm down. Come here, don't move away, don't be a pussy. You're a sissy, Santiago, you're a sissy, a little runt. What am I going to have to do to you, eh? How am I gonna punish you?'

'It's punishment enough to live with this. To live like I live, Alejandro. You know how valuable my work at the Castillo is. We have the same objectives, no? She always says it: "where we come from doesn't matter if our objectives are the same". What's this in comparison to what we've achieved? It doesn't mean anything. I already punish myself, I already find time for whipping and chains, don't suffer for me. We fight for the same things, don't throw everything away for this.'

'Not only are you riddled with AIDS but on top of that you're a disgusting freak, and a hypocrite. How shameless! Has no one ever told you that lying is a sin, that being deceptive is bad, that lies distance us from God?'

'I don't know what you mean.'

'You haven't turned up at the Castillo for a while, so don't come to me now telling me that you give a shit about it all. It's because you don't want to work with my lot, right? Brutes, beasts, more like animals than humans, too physical, too aggressive. We have no complexes when it comes to showing our flesh and you can't stand that. You see a man, and the vein on your temple swells and the drops of sweat run down your forehead and slide down your cheek, you soak your entire shirt, you swell with shame. You look down on us, you look down on everything we do, you despise us and, what's worse, you think we don't realise it, that you think we're all dickheads, that we don't know how far your delusions of grandeur and your egotistical, childish narcissism go. Everything about us seems wrong to you because we get things done, and anything that strays from your plans must be declared an abomination. You think you're above everything and everyone... and you don't even realise, Santiago, that you're just a big fucking coward, that you only have power because my guys are there to do the dirty work, execute your words, put them into practice!'

'We have our differences, sure. But everything else you're saying is nothing but delusional.'

'Delusional, Santiago? You can't stand us! And I know it! I've watched you die of jealousy every time I get close to her. You're funny eh, a faggot who's jealous because his female boss is giving more attention to another guy. Your eyes are always full of contempt. When have you ever bothered to try and understand what motivates us, to get to know us better? Have you ever made an effort to talk to us? You've only tried to substitute our words, change the lexicon. Have you ever been interested in our motives, why we speak the way we speak, the story behind our symbols?'

'I'll say it again, your accusations are ungrounded.'

'Would you prefer small cuts with the knife, nice and slow? Or a quick, painless, aseptic beating, like your self-conscious fucks? Would it turn you on if I put out my cigarette on your back? And watch it, I haven't laid a hand on you yet, so wash your mouth out before you answer me. And don't lie again. Have I already told you I can't stand it when you lie to me?'

'I don't understand what's holding you back.'

Alejandro paused, taking a moment to appear as if he were reflecting on something.

'I've had an idea! And wow, what an idea! Let's see if you understand. First, I'll explain what the main differences are between your project and mine, Santiago. The big differences between my kind and your kind. Let's see if you'll finally comprehend our superiority! The idea of dying has never posed us a problem. We wouldn't just die in any old circumstances, we're not imbeciles, we're not just ready to die during, before or after a football game. But we are ready to die for the dead. We are ready to die for justice. That's called passion, passion for a cause. War and honour.'

'I don't think you need me to kill, nor do I want to play at being kamikaze. Why are you explaining yourself so much? Why does it matter to you that I understand you?'

'Because men depend on their representations, on their ideas, it doesn't matter if they are unaware of it. Ideas are what makes the world go round, Santiago, and ideas are transmitted with words. That's why I need you... and that's why I'm going to forgive you. Don't you see? An image can cause an avalanche of thoughts, a storm in the mind, a bomb, but a word is the only thing that forces us to accept a reality as it is. Without words and without symbols we do not win, and you know how to deal with words.'

'I've only ever wanted to put my words out there. I'm not going to get involved in any games to beautify yours.'

'Did you not just say we were the same? The only way out

when the world looks like it's wrapped up in a spiral of degeneration is through the beauty of nature, language, words. Words build the house, they extend a homeland out to all of us, they reveal themselves to us, appearing and reappearing in truth as nothing else can do like the secret of language. Jünger taught me that. The forest is home, homeland, secret. *Heim, Heimat, Hiemlich.* Everything starts from the same place.'

'You only like him because he's German and sounds German, so he fits into all your vapid aesthetic pretensions, he satisfies your need to collect war figures. Jünger hated Hitler, he looked at the Reich in horror, he would hate everything you stand for. He was a man of letters, you're just mediocre.'

'I'm a lot like you then.'

'You and I are nothing alike.'

'You're wrong, Santiago, I'm a lot like you, I'm just less afraid. I'm a scholar, like you, I'm just not arrogant like you are. I carry around so many readings that are completely useless to me because I don't know how to build things with words: nobody has ever taught me how to use them as a weapon. You know how, and I'm ready to forget about all of this, to turn a blind eye, unite forces.'

'And what if you just hit me now? Your days in the organisation are numbered anyway. None of your images have a place in the world that the Captain wants to construct: she's distancing herself from you. Soon she's going to announce that her organisation condemns all violence, violence committed by radicals that don't form part of the Castillo. She'll speak of you as an infiltrator, an intruder, a mole. She'll give the police your name. What would I gain by uniting with a criminal?'

'You are so naïve.'

'That's not the word I'd use.'

Alejandro became exasperated, chained another cigarette,

sat uncomfortably on my doorstep, patted the space at his side. When he saw that I didn't move, he asked me to sit down. When he saw that I didn't, he yelled two or three times at me to do it until I obeyed. His voice was already that of a deranged man. He offered me a cigarette again, which, out of obligation, I accepted. He calmed down, inhaled and exhaled slowly, and his smile returned. He looked at me almost tenderly.

'You don't understand me. I want you understand me. Do I have to hiss with the deceitfulness typical of pedants, your fucking speciality? Don't laugh! I know you understand me. You already know the story of *Antigone*: there's the lifeless body of Polynices, the dead brother, son of Oedipus and Jocasta. Antigone, a good sister, wants to carry out the funeral rites. The two sides were very clear: on one side is human law, a human creation, the political relationship that man grants to cities when he builds them. And on the other is divine law, a law that exists within the family and where transcendence beyond death is found. The conflict? A dead boy. A dead boy whose remains the arbitrary human laws would not allow to be buried. The divine law is natural law. It has a feminine component, and it takes care of the house and the family. That's its place. Human law takes care of public affairs and is virile, masculine. Woman interprets the law of man as brutality and man the law of woman as insubordination: they are two different logics that come into conflict. Here, it's not so important to think of everything as a war between the sexes, as if we thought about it that way, well, we already know who would win. I can identify with Antigone, but that doesn't mean I'm queer, do you get me? I identify with her because she has to rebel. She can't not! Her parents are dead, she will never have another brother again. She could have another child, she could have another husband, but she will never have another brother, so she must perform his funeral rites. This is a pure, spiritual, natural relationship that allows us to talk about the conflict between many things: the individual and the State, the family, blood, race, the community by natural belonging, the singular and the universal, the particular and the whole. Antigone was the first rebel: she did not accept the authority that violated divine law.'

'I'm not following, Alejandro.'

'It's very simple. I want you to understand what this myth teaches us. From the very moment that someone violates divine law, natural law, the order from which things should never have shifted, all rebellion is justified. All our acts are forgiven, because an authority that violates divine law is unacceptable and illegitimate and is condemned to burn. What I want, Santiago, is to show this to the world, to expose it: no decree of mortals can take precedence over the unwritten and immutable laws of God. Do you remember those lines, Santiago? Those laws are not from today or yesterday but have existed since forever and no one knows what time they date back to. And you see what remains? Degeneration, death, homogenisation, neon screens that replace churches, and prostituted churches hanging adverts for the latest poisonous shit that's come out on Netflix. When we ran through the burning streets of Madrid, between body and body, riot van and riot van, a kid passed through pedalling away on his bike to supply some gentleman stuffed with alprazolam his daily dose of junk food, all while Madrid was in flames! The flames only say one thing: the world deserves to burn. And people will perceive it with much more sympathy than you think.'

'Nobody wants to see a policeman die. You can't feel sympathy after that. And why don't you kill me if I too have infringed divine law?'

'The guy didn't die! It was a miracle, they saved him. We never wanted a policeman to die, we're not idiots.'

'It wouldn't be the first time that one ended up dead. Or do you not want to talk about Palomino?'

'You know that was an accident. Fear makes it impossible to see clearly. They beat him up, the really rough guys... all for a mistake he had made in self-defence. Don't bring that up, it wasn't even me. It wasn't planned. We're talking about the other day here, the demonstration, don't you remember? We can put up with broken benches, bus shelters, bollards, damage to public property, whatever you want. But not the direct responsibility of a death.'

'You've never been close, you've never seen it coming? Because it's a very fine line, Alejandro, and in two moves you cross that line. I'll ask again: do you have blood on your hands?'

'Have a little more respect. About not killing you in particular... even God, from time to time, makes exceptions. Forgiveness comes to all who deserve it. I know that sodomy is a very big blot, written with ink that is difficult to erase, but isn't God merciful, Santiago? Isn't his love infinite? I'll intercede for you, if necessary. He dictates to me, I obey.'

'Do you believe that salvation will come for my actions, do you believe in the structure of a great trial? I think, and it comforts me to think so, that all those futures are already written. You knew from the start that we were enemies. I've always believed that you could not win if I won, that my victory condemned yours, and now you offer me your hand. It's incomprehensible.'

'Finally you admit it! Finally a little bit of sincerity! Thank you! I'm not asking you for anything Santiago. You still don't understand. All I wanted was for you to understand me. You're a fucking degenerate, and I could kill you right here and now. I'd come to beat you up. I didn't even know it was you, but I feel like doing it you know. But I'm not going to touch you. I just want to save your suffering. You belong to me. And on top of that, you're smart, I want your words! If you don't give them to me, you won't give them to anyone. I'll spread your words for you. And you can't threaten me, because if you do, everyone will know. Everyone will know what you are, that little word that scares you so much, that you never say, the word you don't want to identify with... all the fascists will know it, all the Nazis will know it, everyone will know it! And what will they do with you then? How will they deal with you? It's up to you! I thought that with your philosophical circumambulations it would be smoother, you would understand it better, the fall would be softened. I'll be direct: you're in my hands, and you're going to obey me.'

And he was right, because from that exact moment he began to govern every aspect of my life. In a particularly sadistic turn of events, which I would not realise until later, I completely accepted his power to handle what came out of my mouth, submitting to it. In reality, it had been days since I had made any contact with the Castillo, but that was irrelevant. If I confess sincerely, which is exactly what I aspire to do, outlining the fairest and most sincere portrait of myself, I have to say that what Alejandro told me reminded me I once had a purpose in this world, that life revolved around my will to transform it, that for a long time I had thought of myself as in possession of the baton, as a magician or even a conductor, enjoying the precision of all the perfectly complementing instruments and singing the melody that I had carefully placed in their throats without using the slightest measure of cruelty. Not only did I accept obedience and become pious, just as I would have done if Alejandro had had the intention of dominating in a broader sense, but I also rejoiced in my sin and doubled the stakes, believing for a moment that our duo, faced with the Captain's lukewarmness and her exhaustion, would be capable of kidnapping the world every Spring, drying up the flowers, making the leaves fall from the trees. I found it devastating that you abandoned me just when the world was beginning to blossom. I began to hate the smell of jacaranda that had struck me in the demonstration, and every flower that revealed its petals to me was, in my eyes, an affront.

But if he had stolen my entire voice, I would have no power to imagine you again. I wished that in taking over my voice, he would leave no trace of me, that I would disappear completely, vanish, and once again you would have to be the one to raise me from lethargy with a violence that had to take place so that I could wake up. Today I no longer understand the need for this revival, what good would it have been? Reviving me would have been useless, even though it was not sweet to be shipwrecked in that ocean. I cursed you and all that would come after. You know that we're reaching the final images; I refuse to get to the end.

Alejandro dragged me along like his lapdog, taking me with him to a bar near the Castillo where we met the rest of the gang. I had not been there before, but I already knew how to camouflage myself, because during the last few nights I had cultivated myself in the fabrics of these bars: the taps, the dirty walls and floors had become my second skin, as had the uncomfortable chairs and the small bathrooms with just enough space for two people to squeeze into. This world of sad bars was like a liminal membrane attached to my body, just as water adhered to the surface of someone who was about to leave it and come into contact with the hostile air, the cold, and the barbarity of the banal. In a cruel spectacle of humiliation, Alejandro introduced me to everyone one by one, knowing full well that I already knew them, that I had already dealt with them – too much, for my liking – that in the Castillo I handled their dossiers, their information, their memberships; it almost required me to bow to them, kneel down, dramatize the reverence. They greeted me as one of their own with shouts and cheers in that strange hypermasculine brotherhood way, where the contempt they all shared intermingled doubtfully with desire. The rubbing of hands and torsos did not signal secret languages, but rather the codification of an enormous homoerotic fantasy, of the image of men who aspired to sublimate some eternal beauty. My perception of them changed in those minutes, and I saw myself almost enraptured, attracted by so many bodies that together asymptotically aspired to a shared and exalted ideal. If their generosity was beauty, and if violence manifested itself as a different expression of power, of the impulses of force, of the spirit, of the will or of desire, I told myself that I too could desire its excesses and see myself recognised in their way of waving their arms, in their blows, in their hands, and in their tensions.

I could never have slid into an environment like this before, and I wondered if something had got worse since I was forced to confront your absence. I always saw myself in a tower, far away, high up, contemplating those bulging arms from the sky. I always saw myself as far away, high up, unattainable, fading slowly as I dictated from a distance. I never had the slightest desire to go down and join their bonfires or distinguish their roars from their cries. I suppose that in that moment I felt more violent and poisoned, as if possessed, aware that in order to move forward and aspire to a purpose, I had to touch, with greater insistence, that part of me that the toxins possessed, extend it and allow it to inoculate each one of my cells, allow it to conquer the territory of my body. Had Alejandro's discourse permeated me so quickly, so soon? Did I really believe his words about the fury and the storm? Everything was happening so quickly that I came to conceive his rhetoric as my invention, and that the seed had always been present in my proposal. Madrid burning down in an afternoon was an omen, perhaps the still frame that would inspire the imitators of the future, but the need to wield all the trembling forces of destruction with many hands would only flourish if, before my words, they had done their job with the land. I realised that I could command the storm of deadly fires, and the defeats I had suffered no longer seemed so painful to me.

I confess that I got drunk and I even admit that I let myself have fun. Among the effects of alcohol when it enters the bloodstream is a certain lack of inhibition, a letting go of all hindrance, a euphoria, impetus, joy. I was accumulating all this while trying to blend in with those monsters, not stray too far from them, pass as just another one of them, the most faithful and complicit to his leader. The place had already officially closed, but the waiter had no qualms about mingling with us, he talked to us about our issues. Those of that day were the biological nation, ethnic substitution, the need to ensure a future for white children. He gave us shots on the house and let us cut lines on his bar. I was unable to distinguish between that bar and any of the bars I began to fall into after you, because the similarities outweighed the differences. Alejandro seemed even happier, more content, smiling; he was even more unbalanced on his feet, his voice was slightly nasal, his tone when he spoke seemed broken, as if rage were going to explode between his random stutters. The others responded with a mixture of obedience and almost erotic rebellion, getting cocky, edging around, and trying to claim a small share of power before then giving up before the leader took it too seriously, relying on little games and childish trifles. I recognised the songs they sang: one was Estirpe Imperial's[*] version of the Russian *Katyusha* song, as a tribute to the Blue Division. I thought about how sad I was, and the song revived some sadness in me: the world was burning, but I listened to the lyrics and only thought about myself, about you, about your absence.

[*] Estirpe Imperial is a Spanish nationalist and fascist rock band, active since 1991.

An angel riding on horseback
Riding with verve and courage
Sings the sad stories
Of a war that's over

Springtime far from my homeland
Springtime far from my love
Springtime without flowers and laughter
Springtime on the banks of the Volkhov

Its waters overlooking the Ladoga
Go on singing this sad song
Sad song of love and war
Sad song of war and love

When the enemy drunkenly advances
Attacking with vodka, without courage
The air shreds louder than with shrapnel
The verses of my Cara al sol.[*]

Cara al sol, *old and new song*
Cara al sol, *the most beautiful hymn*
Cara al sol *and die fighting*
As my homeland asked me to do

If in the struggle I were broken
I would march in the Legion of Honour
I would ride in the guard of the stars,
I would be a part of the best

---

*Cara al Sol (tr. Facing the Sun) is the anthem of the Falange Española de las JONS. The lyrics are usually credited to the leader of the Falange, José Antonio Primo de Rivera.

Now comes the worst part of all, Ramiro, but I have relived all of this to be able to get to this point, to be able to stay calm, to be able to tell myself that I've managed to tell you everything until the end, that nothing has been left behind, so that perhaps one day I will be able to live in peace. It is the part of the story that until now I have pushed into darkness, the part that drags down the rest. You don't know how many times I've told myself since everything, that if that night had never happened, you would have ended up forgiving me, we could have loved each other, you would have found me in some way or another. I have gone over and over these images a thousand times, Ramiro, because I see them every time I close my eyes, but until today I have never been able to put them into words, and to do so I need you to promise me that if I manage to capture them, write them down, even crudely, poorly, that those images burned into my mind will disappear, that I will be released from their control. If only you could promise me that. After he had snorted a line, Alejandro approached me and out of the blue told me he had prepared a surprise, a welcome gift. I replied that I hoped that this wasn't some sort of hazing and he just grinned. You have no idea how much I remember that grin. A few of us – I supposed that, apart from me, those who were left must have trusted him – got into the van, there must have been about seven or eight of us. He started to drive towards the city centre, slowly, without haste, a co-driver sat next to him, trembling, his mobile phone in his hand. I didn't see it, Ramiro, but imagine if I had, if I had seen that figure, the distance slowly dropping, the meters in free fall, little by little, until the number ceased to exist, if I had recognised the app and saw that it was the same one that I used, if you had ever told me about that Fran you met in your first days in the Commune, if I had realised that the same person who had threatened to kill me for being a faggot was the mole that the

179

Captain had placed in your organisation… Ramiro, there are so many things I regret. Because then I saw you from the window of the van, and I wish you had seen me, although you would never have forgiven me then, because you would have known what was to come. I know you couldn't see me, but I urged you to run. I was about to shout out to you to see if you could hear me, risking being the one killed, but I didn't say anything. I kept quiet, remained silent, waited until we parked. Alejandro looked at me, the cigarette in his hand, the grin still on his face. *You can stay here*, he told me, *or you can come and admire the spectacle.* At first, I just sat in the van, watching as everyone else got out. Then I couldn't resist it; I ran out without closing the door and approached them and the alley into which they were following you. I also put up my hood. I watched how, suddenly, a herd of shadows approached you and grabbed your neck without tenderness, pushed you against a container, dragged you along the ground. I heard the only cry of pain that came out of your mouth before they covered it with some tape. I didn't want to get any closer, and from a distance the only thing I heard were the screams, the voices of the guys I was with in chorus: 'fucking faggot', 'AIDS carrier', and from a distance the only thing I saw was a shower of hands, kicks, and words, insistent blows that rained down over and over again on your face until they broke your nose, a rain of blows to your side to break your ribs. Madrid's sky was black and I, a coward, thought that if I just stayed there, contemplating the images, I would never have a reason to feel responsible for that beating. I thought that at some point the blows would stop, I never believed that they would continue to rush over you like a torrent, nor did I contemplate the possibility that their intention had been to take your life away.

I began to see blood amidst the darkness as if the colour red, even in those small quantities, would completely illuminate the city, transforming the world and everything present; there wasn't much, but I knew there was some, and still I didn't go towards you. I was about to scream, Ramiro, I swear I was about to scream, but I didn't. And then they all came running towards me and I thought I was going to be their next victim, but they only told me to get back in the van, told me that we had to go, that you were unconscious and that you would wake up. I chose to believe them. Had anyone seen us? I thought not and I told myself that I was innocent, that I had never laid a hand on you, that I would never have hit you unless you asked me to. I figured that tomorrow, on the news, it would be reported that some sort of neo-Nazi gang had beaten up a young homosexual in the early hours of the morning when he was coming back from a party. Alejandro confirmed the presence of a stranger, a witness who screamed, sounded the alert, and caused everyone to stampede back into the van: he hit the dashboard a few times between insults and prayed that they had not seen the license plate, assuring the others that he had the security cameras in the neighbourhood well locked down.

Driving the van to a remote area, he left everyone to their fate. I preferred to go back alone, and even though I considered going back to where you had been attacked, just to see if you were okay, I didn't deviate from my trajectory. I told myself that tomorrow you would be fine, that tomorrow I could write you a message, talk to you, and that it was impossible that you were not ok. I promised myself, suddenly awake, that I would do everything possible to get us back together, that I would stay away from the Castillo, from Alejandro, from the violence. I told myself that I had never been a part of it, that the seriousness of my guilt could not be measured with similar criteria to theirs. Lying in bed, listening for one more night to the same noises as every night, my pathetic scene of insomnia repeated itself while

I was dying for dawn to grant me the opportunity for hope.

I believe you already know how your story ends.

I am sure you would find something capricious in the way that I have had to imagine us, but I promise you that I couldn't have done it any other way. Whenever I write of Santiago, I do it because I am no longer the person who lived through all those things and, if I could, I would erase my name, my rubbish, my remains, everything that would explain why I ever passed through this world. You, on the other hand, will always look like the image I keep of you. I have tried to revive you, Ramiro, in exactly this way, the way I knew you, because if I think of you I have to think of you as still existing, to act as if you had not died. The only way I can live with myself is to insist that you are alive, and it's as if the things we experienced together are just happening again and again, because they play over and over in my head. There are moments that I will see forever, that repeat themselves over and over: like the moment I realised – watching the news in the same old fucking dive bar – that you had died, but not from the blows, you had died because in the middle of the beating your heart had stopped. From then there was no turning back: you had died and the last image I had of you was already the image, the bleeding silhouette, the shadow of a dead person, without my being aware, without my ever thinking you were dying. In the days following your death I asked myself again and again how Madrid had become nothing but a vast tomb. Now I go over and over all of the details and I imagine what I would change today. I always insist, whenever I talk to you, that you don't blame me, because I didn't go with them, because that's how I make my life more liveable: I try to think, to insist, to repeat that they would have ended up hunting you down anyway, in however many different versions of the same story. I also try to tell myself that punishment and retaliation are legitimate, and have built a whole version of the world in which something like this ends up happening to all those who are like you and do not repent or are not ashamed of what they are. I tell myself that if your heart or your veins were weak, that they might have burst any day in an anxiety attack, and I would never have been able to do anything to avoid it anyway. And it's not like I'm lying, I don't lie to myself, but I don't believe everything I say. I need you to tell me that these thoughts were true, that you forgive me with a caress, as if accepting without verbalising that yes, that I couldn't do anything, how was I going to stop the blows or the torrent or the fists? I am sure that today you would laugh if I told you that we were evicted from the Castillo barely a week after your group was evicted from the Commune. You didn't witness this, so for you the fruit of so much of your labour, the product of your broom, remains alive forever. Every year the same Soviet movies are repeated, someone makes the same sterile comments, and I tell you that Eisenstein didn't invent anything and neither did Marx, but in your eyes the memories of those projections remain and you talk to me. Though in the end you didn't talk to me and ignored each and every one of my messages; now, you talk to me. Perhaps you would talk to me again, Ramiro, if I told you that I was no longer involved with those who killed you, and then you would take my word away when I commented that I still, inevitably, ran into them from time to time. A memory does not end, but rather abandons you, it leaves you behind, but the screams are still distinguishable, and the footprints follow you. I still have not abandoned you, listen to me, because while all of this is rushing through my mind and I think about the nights I spent with you, I sometimes still hear your moans. I promise you that I can imagine the timbre and the volume exactly as it was and the image is so clear, so beautiful, that I confess to having masturbated to the memory. Ramiro, now that you are not here,

I can tell you about how since that day in the demonstration I have masturbated compulsively thinking about you. I don't know if I am cruel, I don't know if it is cruel, but I think you would have done the same, and I feel that since that day, you thought of me too. Sometimes, if I fall even deeper and recreate that day in my head again, and even with your death I still feel that you think of me. I do not want to erase that last image of you, disfigured and broken, decomposed. I want to modify it and make it another, forge my very own last image of you like a mechanism that is activated and does not stop, conceive it as violence is conceived. It's all so banal Ramiro, so banal. I am sure that you would also have lost faith, as we all do over time, and you would realise how nice it is to live among the disbelievers, to take everything in from a distance. There were no detainees when the police evacuated the Commune building. I followed the whole process carefully, because my days were enormously empty, exhausting, and hollow. Where your Commune used to be, Ramiro, they have built a modern hostel for young people, with a self-check-in, buffet breakfast, cafe bar, sun terrace, air conditioning, events, a pool on the roof, a virtual reality room, a mini-cinema, a foodie restaurant with 'traditional' food from Madrid and brunch, vertical gardens, and lots of sadness. I can imagine your laugh. I dream that that laughter would come from a special kind of confused rage, like a smile that you don't fully believe, that seems fake, and that nevertheless appears and reappears. I dream that I finally make you laugh and you tell me that all this time you've been playing dead because you really wanted me to find the perfect joke, the right joke, the right word to revive you. And your absence hurts me a lot because you have missed so many things. Since you've been gone Afghanistan has exploded, our parliamentary right speaks of the Spanish solar empire, and European presidents announce that their duty is to anticipate and protect from irregular migratory flows that would endanger their peoples. Their advisers speak of a migratory tsunami that must be prevented at all costs and even the social democrats, those you criticised so much when the revisionists governed, whilst not saying the same thing, raise the borders just as high. The communists today speak like me, everyone today speaks like me, repeating the slogans that I popularised: revolt against the modern world, rise in a world of ruins. Think about it, Ramiro, because you would have ended up waking up too.

I would like to enjoy all of this, but I can't, and it hurts me not to have you by my side to contemplate my great semantic empire: I no longer need to direct all the instruments of a tiny radical organisation, of a small group, Ramiro, because my discourse is everywhere, my voice is in all voices and the whole world speaks my language.

I'm beginning to believe, Ramiro, that it's useless to be the owner of a city or the master of words if you don't have someone to share it with, if you can't extend the conversation a little longer. I think that this is the poison that you offered me, and I was anxious of the impossibility of knowing how to live without you. I think about what your habits were and try to imitate them. When I manage to get out of bed, I go to bars and I like to stay until they close. I no longer enjoy getting passionate about a cause as I could when I was with you; I have lost anything resembling sexual desire, or at least sexual desire for other bodies, but I would not dare to say that you've cured me, because I suppose that I am still sick with you. I've told you before: the only thing that still excites me is your memory, your images, from time to time my words describing those images. I hope with them you can forgive me.

The only thing that no longer seems violent to me is trying to contemplate the world through your eyes, thinking of my own as if I had removed yours and placed them in my head. I have searched the cemetery for your corpse, I have dug up all the earth from your tomb with my hands, hands that I have clumsily ripped off and replaced with yours. I go out partying to the places you took me, and I try to come back at the same time you came back. I have not yet dared to go to your house, to try to open the door with your key, to search your room, and I have changed my phone number so that your flatmates will not contact me. I haven't been summoned by the police, so I'm glad they didn't suspect me for your murder. Something in me wants to believe that they think me incapable, that they know how much I really loved you. Sometimes I attempt to walk the route of the demonstration, the last day we spoke, and I still keep your messages asking me to accompany you as if they were treasure; those messages were so clumsily ignorant, Ramiro, so beautiful. I walk the demonstration just as you did, starting at Atocha and heading up to Cibeles, then passing through Gran Vía. Then I walk the route that I took, that I lived. I wait for a long time in Plaza de España before then making my way up to Callao. Sometimes I wander and look for myself closer to Plaza del Dos de Mayo. People are surprised to see me run, leap, and jump, Ramiro, but I can remember the images so clearly, and when I think of the fire, I can still imagine the flames are alive today, and that what prevents me from breathing is the smoke, that the smoke is to blame for my asphyxiation. I pace the streets looking for you, I search for you in the churches, I search for you in the parks. Tell me, Ramiro, do you want me to find you? I go to the alley where they killed you and I tried to find the exact spot from which I watched the whole scene, but I find it impossible to do. I think I have finally managed to exorcise the image, the first of my goals: now I close my eyes and no longer think of blood, crooked noses, or stopping hearts. I close my eyes and think only of you. I have looked for you everywhere in this city, I have walked all its streets, but until now I had not realised that maybe I could only find you from above. I've heard that from the roof of the new hotel on Calle Encomienda, at certain hours of the day you can see a man being devoured by a hurricane of pigeons.

AUTHOR'S NOTE

I finished writing this novel on the 29th of August 2021. Just a few days later, I found out that the organisation that inspired the Castillo (a kind of ghostly copy) had once again occupied what were, during the time of NO-DO (a news organisation that produced propaganda during the Franco era), the RTVE headquarters, just like they had occupied them in 2016. That is, they reconquered the very same place in which a large part of this text takes place. To focus too much on this in these final pages would give the last words in this book a bitter taste. I am glad that they are condemned, at least for now, to relative irrelevance. I don't think we should give them too much attention. I believe they're like cats: a plague, yes, but above all a being that seeks to subjugate its human, asking for food at five in the morning and then insisting on eating a little earlier the next day upon seeing that its first attempt bore fruit. If one ignores their existence for long enough, they will die as they can't stand not being the centre of attention. The worrying thing, however, is not their existence: the worrying thing is that their discourse exists within everyone else, that their voice is found in all voices, and that the whole world speaks their language. The left will never win if they try to elaborate great images of cities devastated by fear and desolation – especially when these images do not correspond to reality – because the discourse of order and exploitation of fear is always better spun by those who carry it in their blood. This author's note is a space in which I have been allowed to impart some knowledge or ideas, but my intention with this book was never to offer the key for the left to win, nor even to describe with surgical precision the components of an all too real extreme right: the mirrors of fiction exaggerate and reduce; what I tell here, after all, is a rather small story of love and violence.

The organisations that appear in this book are fictional versions of real organisations. The facts, too, are fictionalised. There was never a meeting between two protests, the dates don't add up, Madrid never burned in this way, and a curfew was never enforced. I cherish with respect and love my memories of the Caja Roja and the Iniciativa Comunista, organisations in which I was a pre-militant at the age of fifteen and sixteen and where I published in one of its monographs on working women and imperialism. Apart from the Captain, none of the people in this book exist in the real world. If, by chance, I am mistaken and they do exist, and something I have written reminds anyone of someone real, of flesh and blood, then that would be a simple coincidence of the imagination that has somehow made me come to know someone without ever knowing them.

29th August 2021

TRANSLATOR'S NOTE

Whilst *Madrid Will be Their Tomb* is a book about Spanish politics and two men from the country's capital, as I write right now it could be a book about any Western European country's politics, about two men from any Western European city. As an adopted *madrileña* and someone who lives, literally, a stone's throw from where the clash of demonstrations takes place, I have come to understand all too well what is festering in this city's sewers, swelling its cement, infecting its arteries: it is something that is also festering on the shores of the country in which I was born, swelling its green, rolling hills and infecting its rivers. When I began my translation of the novel in January 2023, British politics was massively unstable (arguably, it still is), fuelled by a disgusting rhetoric around immigration and the attempt to convince the British public that Brexit was, or at least would be, a roaring success. Whilst they are set in different contexts, you can see why translating some of Duval's more unsavoury characters' words was difficult.

As my work on the translation went on, my focus was drawn away from the politics of the country I once called home, the United Kingdom, and towards the politics of Spain when during the local elections of 28th May 2023, the extreme right reared its ugly head and prompted the centre-left PSOE's leader to call a snap general election on the 23rd of July 2023. In the run up to the election the news, social media and papers were filled with horrendous and shameful discourse from the extreme right, specifically regarding women's and LGBTQI+ rights. This was discourse that once again meant translating some of Duval's more unsavoury characters' words was all too close to home.

As Duval explains in her author's note, *Madrid Will be Their Tomb* was never intended to be a book that would 'offer the key for the left to win, nor even to describe with surgical precision the components of an all too real extreme right', rather what she intended to do was write a 'rather small story of love and violence', and this is exactly what she does. However, with *Madrid Will be Their Tomb*, Duval does remind us that in an increasing number of Western European countries, something is festering in our cities' sewers, swelling its cement, infecting its arteries, and that something will continue to do so if we do not confront it.

1st August 2023